Set in 1969, Donovan's groundbreaking work centers on Davy Ross, a lonely thirteen-year-old boy. When his grandmother dies, Davy must move to Manhattan to live with his estranged mother. Between alcohol-infused lectures about her self-sacrifice and awkward visits with his distant father, Davy's only comfort is his beloved dachshund Fred. Things start to look up when he and a boy from school become friends. But when their relationship takes an unexpected physical turn, Davy struggles to understand what happened and what it might mean.

John Donovan was a novelist, a playwright, and a former president of the Children's Book Council. *I'll Get There. It Better Be Worth the Trip.* was originally published in 1969 and reprinted by Dell in 1973.

I'll

get

there.

It better be

worth

the trip.

I'll

get

there.

It better be

worth

the trip.

40TH ANNIVERSARY EDITION

J O H N   D O N O V A N

flux
™
Woodbury, Minnesota

First hardcover edition published 1969 by Harper & Row
First paperback edition published 1972 by Harper & Row

First Flux edition 2010
First printing, 2010

Cover design by Ellen Dahl
Cover image © Image Source/PunchStock

Flux, an imprint of Llewellyn Worldwide Ltd.

This is a work of fiction. Names, characters, places, and incidents are either the product of the author's imagination or are used fictitiously, and any resemblance to actual persons, living or dead, business establishments, events, or locales is entirely coincidental. Cover models used for illustrative purposes only and may not endorse or represent the book's subject.

Library of Congress Cataloging-in-Publication Data
Donovan, John, 1929–1992.
  I'll get there, it better be worth the trip: 40th anniversary edition
/ John Donovan.—1st Flux ed.
    p. cm.
  Summary: While trying to cope with his alcoholic mother and absent
father, a lonely New York City teenager develops a confusing crush on
another boy.
  ISBN 978-0-7387-2134-7
  [1. Friendship—Fiction. 2. Homosexuality—Fiction.
3. Alcoholism—Fiction. 4. New York (N.Y.)—History—20th
century—Fiction.] I. Title. II. Title: I will get there, it better be
worth the trip.
  PZ7.D7228Il 2010
  [Fic]—dc22

                                    2010014266

                            Flux
            A Division of Llewellyn Worldwide Ltd.
                    2143 Wooddale Drive
                  Woodbury, MN 55125-2989
                      www.fluxnow.com

            Printed in the United States of America

What a Trip

Dear John,

By the time I met Davy in these pages, I was already surrounded by the best books. Thanks to the magical boxes you sent several times a year, my world was alive with *The Catcher in the Rye, Doctor Doolittle, Harriet the Spy, The Mad Scientists' Club.* I believed as much in those characters enlivening the pages as I did in what was supposedly real beyond their stories—even more.

That's the way it is with books sometimes. They can mean more than actual moments because they might stay in our minds forever.

When *I'll Get There...* arrived, there was something instantly different about it. Not because Davy wasn't cool or collected, or that he'd lost so much in life already. The more he thought about and felt what was happening around him, the more I did too. He was tender, he was deep. He was lost, not fake. His divorced parents were each a mess for their own reasons.

But he had Fred, most excellent dachshund, and their connection meant pretty much everything. Until Davy met

Altschuler at school, when a whole different part of life began.

I remember asking you once, have you ever been in love? Only about fifty times, you answered. We laughed and rushed through the New York City streets on the way to the theater. You introduced me to ballet, to drama, to opera, your hunger to taste the stinging, the sweet, everything.

When you died I thought, like Davy, that my heart could not bridge another separation. Yet life rarely offers the opportunity to go back to a world made exquisite with meaning, the world you brought into existence with *I'll Get There* .... How lucky we are to have you back in these pages.

My love and missing you always.

Your niece,
Stacey Donovan

New York City

1969

one

The limousine drives up in front of the house. I am in the jump seat by the door closest to the sidewalk, so I open the door and fumble with the seat I was sitting on. I'm not getting anywhere with it.

"I'll take care of that, sir," the driver says. He pounces out of the car and puts his hand on the door I opened. "Don't you bother with that, Mr. Ross," he says, emphatically this time.

"I can get it," I say. "I'm sure I can." I don't like him. He needs a haircut in the worst way. Not that I ordinarily care about haircuts, but for the limousine driver at my grandmother's funeral, I thought they could at least have given us a guy who had had his hair cut.

"Let him do it, Davy." That is my mother. "We're not all of us mechanics." Then she laughs. Everyone looks at her, and she stops.

"There we go, sir." The driver folds the seat in half a second. I sort of smile at him as though I am thanking him. "Nothing to it, sir," he says. The bastard. All that "sir" business. I don't know what he takes me for. Twice before, once at a fancy restaurant and once when I opened a savings account in a bank, guys had called me "sir." I thought it was pretty phony then, and I still do. This guy working for the funeral home takes the prize though. He must have called me "sir" about twenty times so far this morning. Maybe I'll get used to it later. Maybe when I'm fourteen. I doubt it.

Everyone files out of the car and onto the front porch. The driver is all smiles and has I'll-be-seeing-you-in-rosier-circumstances looks, so I don't even say good-bye to him. Everyone looks at me, and I realize I am supposed to open the door. As soon as I put in the key, old Fred lets out a howl from the inside, and I yell, "It's OK, Fred. It's just me." He stops barking right away, and I can hear him near the door, sniffing away. I wait just a minute before I open the door because I think Fred gets a lot of pleasure from sniffing like that. It gives him a few seconds to decide who's going to be coming through the door. Then I open the door, and Fred jumps on my legs. He gets so excited that he squirts on the floor.

"Isn't he trained?" my mother asks.

"Oh, sure. He's just glad to see me. That's all."

My mother walks past Fred as though he weren't there, and then my uncle and aunt come in, and then my great-aunt and her daughter, or daughter-in-law, I could never figure out which, but I sort of like her because she always kisses me in a friendly way, even though we only see each other on big family occasions. My other uncle, the one from Los Angeles who isn't married, comes in last. He's like a stranger. The only thing I remember about him until now is that when I was a little kid he told me not to eat some potato chips on my grandmother's table one Sunday night before supper. He said there wouldn't be enough for everyone else if I did. Needless to say, since this is my only connection with Uncle Jess, he never held a top position in my people book. But this time he was OK. I felt sorry for him more than for anyone else. He cried very hard when he saw my grandmother in her casket. He got all riled up and said he should have been coming East every year to see her, and that he had wanted to come up to Boston the last time he was in New York, but he couldn't because if he didn't get to London some terrible thing would happen, and it happened anyway, so what was the point. Uncle Jess used to send Grandmother a check every month. He didn't have time to write letters though, and now he felt guilty as hell. He needn't have, I think. Grandmother didn't have much to say about Uncle Jess, just about things that happened a long time ago when he was in high school or growing up. He's some kind of model. He had his nose straightened, and his hair is all fixed up to look blond. Old Fred keeps sniffing at him, but he hasn't licked him. I don't think Fred knows yet whether Uncle Jess wants to be licked. Dachshunds are like that. They respect you if you are not a big dog-lover. If you are though, watch out!

Fred keeps running back and forth from me to all the

people. Then I know I'm going to cry. He's looking for my grandmother. I know it sure as anything. He keeps running around to everyone, and each time he sniffs and then runs back to me and jumps up. I hold him close two or three times, but he pops right out of my arms and runs around again. He finally goes to the door and just looks at it.

"He has to make, David," my mother says. Big dog-lover.

"I don't think so." I have a hard time getting that out because Fred has shaken me up now. Grandmother went away for two or three days now and then. Fred didn't like it when she was away. He didn't like it when I was away either. Sometimes I would go to New York for the weekend to visit my mother, and once I went to Canada for a couple of weeks with my father on his vacation, and each time old Fred thought he was being deserted. But then each time I came back. And Grandmother came back. That is the difference this time. Fred knows she isn't coming back. He looks at me and cries. Oh, God, that hurts. He has this short whine, and he uses it when he wants attention or when something is hurting him. It's that whine Fred is using at the door, only it seems to me to be deeper. That does it. I can't take it any more, so I run over to old Fred and fall right down there with him in front of the door, and I bawl my head off. We both do, and once I start I can't stop. It gets louder and louder, and I have a hard time catching my breath, and my ribs start to ache. Poor Fred. He just keeps crying too. Everyone in the room stands there, dumbfounded I guess. Finally Mother kneels down next to me to pull me up.

"Don't do that, Helen," Aunt Louise says. "It's better this way."

"Oh, my poor baby," Mother says. She runs her hands over my back. I look up at her. Her eyes are moist, and I throw both myself and Fred, I guess, into her arms. In a minute I stop bawling and calm down a little bit, so I pull away from Mother. Fred isn't whining any more either, so I guess that crisis has passed. Everyone is staring at me as though I am a patient who has just come out of ether.

"I'm sorry," I say.

They all say No, No, No and smile encouragingly, so I begin to feel a little dopey. There isn't anything to say, so I breathe deeply once and get up from the floor.

"Fred and I will take a run, I guess." Fred won't let me get two inches away from him now, so there is no problem in getting him out the front door. Sometimes he is reluctant, especially if he thinks there might be some food waiting to be begged for. Not now though. Poor Fred. I wish he could talk or let me know in some way he understands all the stuff I say to him.

two

It is a good thing that I go out when I do because I know that they are all itching to get on with the inevitable conversation and that as long as I am in the room, or in the house even, they will just sit there being polite, trying not to hurt my feelings, and no one will say what everyone has on his mind. What becomes of me? I'm sure they want to get the whole thing settled in two or three hours. They won't sit in the same room again until the next person in the family dies. If they want to get something talked out all together, it's now or not at all. I am glad to be away from them anyway. I don't really have anything to *say* to any of them. There aren't many adults I have anything to *say* to, and now there is one less, with Grandmother dead.

Our house is right near the beach, and whether I want to or not, that's where Fred and I go to have a run. He loves the beach for two good reasons. The first is digging. He digs like a maniac. People are always stopping to stare at him on the beach, and at least once a week someone asks me if I know why Fred digs like that. They don't believe me when I tell them I know why, so they tell me anyway—that his ancestors were badger hunters and that's why dachshunds scratch so furiously at the earth and the sand. I don't tell them I know all about this any longer. People like to think they are instructive. What the hell. If it makes them feel useful, I am glad to listen.

The second reason Fred zips over to the beach at the least provocation is dead fish. Nothing makes Fred happier than a smelly dead fish. And he's really got a nose for them. To tell the truth, I don't much like it when Fred throws himself all over the fish, not because it isn't funny to see him do it—it is—but because of later. He walks around smelling like a mackerel for two days after, and, to tell the truth, I would be just as happy to keep him at a distance when that happens. Except who can keep a big lover like Fred at a distance? He goes crazy just to give me a kiss whenever I come home.

Fred and I run along the beach for a few minutes. He's still acting as though he knows something is up. Ordinarily he would be scratching away by this time or would have his nose up in the air, sniffing for a fish. Not today. He sticks close to me. He never gets more than two feet in front of me, and when he gets even that far, he keeps looking back to check if I am still there. Usually I'm just jogging along, and Fred is a hundred yards ahead of me. I find a piece of wood and put it right in front of Fred's face. Then I toss it about fifteen feet in front of him.

"Go get it, Fred! Bring it to Dave!"

Fred looks at me as though I'm crazy, so I just sit down on the sand. Fred sits right down too, and I rub him under the muzzle and then his neck. He purrs.

"You're not a cat, Fred. Or maybe you are. Are you half cat, Fred?" He looks up at me, his dumb face begging for a kiss, so I bend over and pull him into my lap. He cradles his head under my chin, and in two seconds his eyes are closed and he's breathing heavily with the kind of instant and total sleep Fred seems able to fall into every time he's contented. I laugh a little and fall back on the sand. No one is on the beach. It is the middle of October, and the sun is bright and comfortable. I wonder why no one else is here on a lovely day like today until I remember it is the middle of the week and most people are working or at school. Fred half opens his eyes when I fall back, makes a very easy adjustment to my new position, and is sound asleep again in half a second. I hold my arms around him so he won't fall off my chest, and he sighs deeply. That was just the right thing to do, and I'm happy I did it. I think I fell asleep then too.

Not for long. Fred and I wake with a start. A wave has cracked not too far away and made a noise different from the steady, even breaking of most of the waves. Fred is really mad, and he jumps out of my arms and dashes to the edge of the water. He barks at the ocean.

"Give it hell, Fred," I shout. And Fred barks again and

again. Another wave breaks gently, and Fred barks at it before running back to me.

"Good dog! Where does the sea get off—interrupting our sleep?" I toss Fred's head around a little bit, from hand to hand, and he jumps up, more playful than when we first came to the beach.

"That's the good boy," I urge him on. I pick up another small piece of driftwood and toss it out. Fred chases it and brings it back. We do this four or five times until Fred gets bored with it and begins to dig. Before you know it he has pushed a pile of sand through his hind legs and has a big hole ready for who knows what. In the summer Fred curls up in the holes he digs because they are cooler than the top sand. Not now though. He seems to be looking for a clam, which probably has buried itself deep when hearing Fred scratch away. I have never known him to get a clam in this way, but people are always telling me that's one of the reasons for digging. People and their facts.

Fred and I mess around some more, and then I guess that it's time to go home.

"OK, friend, now's the time. It's now or never."

Fred scratches away again and then squats to do his business. He looks at me for approval while he's doing it, so I say, "That's a good boy. Oh, that's marvelous. Fred's a good dog." I guess he's pleased because when he's finished, he trots over and brushes by my leg.

three

I never thought much about my grandmother. I came to live with her when I was about five, before I began going to school, and I don't think that kids of five *think* too much anyway. I knew that most of the boys and girls I met at school lived with their parents. But they all had grandparents, and they occasionally talked about all the money they got from them on their birthdays and the good places their grandparents took them. None of them talked about their grandparents as though they really knew them, or even wanted to. I may have been a little embarrassed when I asked some kids to come home with me after school for the afternoon and introduced them to Grandmother and then waited for the question they all asked in their own ways. It is really funny to realize how tactful little kids can be in a blunt way. My favorite kid on this was Rosemary Mayer, who always had on neat dresses and did a lot of homework.

When I introduced her to Grandmother, Rosemary turned to me and said, "And your parents, Mr. and Mrs. Ross, are they traveling in Europe?" That's pretty good for a seven-year-old kid.

The thing about Grandmother was how orderly she was. Everything had a place and fit into its proper place or it was out—she'd have nothing to do with it, or she'd forget it if she could. She was a great one for saying "Don't pay any attention" when some bum would come up to us on the street in Boston, asking for money. Or if something terrible happened, like the time I threw a metal compass at some kid I was mad at in school, she would pretend it had never happened after I had had my punishment, not because she was ashamed of me or anything like that, but just because it was too rough on her to think of what I was really doing when I did this terrible thing to that guy. I got nervous about myself after that episode. I can't even remember what I was mad at now, but I certainly know that I have a temper. I really wanted to talk with her about this, but every time I brought it up even indirectly, she cut me off with a look.

When I look back over it now, it must have been pretty rough on Grandmother. I don't know how old she was, but I guess she was over sixty. And here she was with this boy about to go into school when she must have been getting ready to relax and take things easy for life, as easy as she could anyway. Like I said, everything in her house had a particular spot, and God help anyone who moved it. Me especially. When I was a little kid, I naturally picked up a lot of things to examine them. This used to drive Grandmother buggy, and the buggier she got, the more things I picked up. First it was ashtrays. I figured it didn't make any difference if I broke one because Grandmother didn't smoke and always emptied ashtrays at the end of each cigarette when some visitor came. This was her way of curtailing the smoking of a second cigarette. But if that didn't work, she opened all the windows in the room where the smoker was sitting, and he usually got the hint. Some people didn't though, and Grandmother caught a few colds as a result.

I liked to pick up a lot of other things too, and it wasn't long before all her stuff was either locked up or put up so high that I would have needed a ladder to reach it. This is what I mean by how rough it must have been on her. She had laid out her house without kids in mind, then had to lay it out again with me in mind. She didn't make a great big thing of it though. She just did it. It was only a year or so before she died that she began to bring things out in the open again. I guess she never got a chance to be old in the way most people are.

She always tried to ask me questions about schoolwork and friends. She worked very hard at being a good parent. She never had the pleasure of being a grandparent. Poor good girl. Now she never will.

It was Grandmother who realized first that she was never going to bring it off and that with her and me it would always be a friendly, but awkward situation. When it got close to my eighth birthday, she said, "David, I'm not going to ask what you want this year. Is that all right?" I didn't know what to make of what she said, so I just nodded. I had gotten a twenty-five-dollar birthday check from my father that morning, so it didn't make much difference what else I got.

Two days later, on my actual birthday, when I came home from school, I heard a funny noise in the kitchen. I ran back to see what it was. There was Grandmother bending over a box filled with newspapers, stroking about ten inches of black dachshund. It was Fred. She picked him up and handed him to me.

"Happy birthday, David."

My eyes must have gotten as wide as two tennis balls. I reached over to get Fred. He was wiggling in Grandmother's hands. As I held him to me he squirted all over my jacket. Grandmother and I laughed. Fred, the nut, he just licked away at my face.

four

I don't know how long Fred and I have been gone from the house, but it is long enough for there to be tension in the air when we get back. I can see through the front windows that they are sitting around in the living room. Mother has got out of her black dress and is wearing pants. Everyone else looks somber though, so Mother looks funny. I can hear a lot of loud talk long before I reach the house, but it isn't clear from the street whether there is an argument or a party. It doesn't take long for me to find out.

"What do you think New York is?" I hear Mother shout. "If you'd come over to see me more than once every five years, you'd know what a perfectly lovely, friendly, marvelous place New York can be!"

I am right outside the door now.

"David isn't a city boy. It's unfair to him to make a change now."

"He won't be going to Russia!"

I am going to turn away, but Fred is jumping on the door, scratching away, and they hear him. Silence. Then Uncle Jess opens the door.

"Hi," I say. I try very hard to seem out of breath, as if maybe I had just run up onto the porch. I don't want any of them to think I stand around listening to their dumb arguments. Personally I couldn't care one hoot what they argue about. Boy, are they quiet when Fred and I come in. Mother smiles at me as though I'm some object she is thinking of buying in a store. Aunt Louise looks wan and frightened, and my great-aunt looks ossified.

"Have a good run, Davy?" Uncle Jess finally asks.

"Oh, sure."

Fred lopes around from person to person, gets no encouragement from anyone, and finally throws himself down over my feet. I am standing there, no more than two or three feet inside the door, with Uncle Jess standing next to me, and the quiet is like you can serve it.

"Did I interrupt?" I finally ask.

No, No, No, they all say, and I get the feeling that everyone feels sorry for me, which I don't like at all. I shift my feet, and Fred looks at me as though I've got nerve to disturb him.

"I was thinking," I begin, "with Grandmother dead, I guess you're all worried about me. Where I'll live, I mean."

They fall all over themselves trying to say No again. I don't know what makes them so embarrassed. Two minutes ago they were screaming at each other about this very subject, and now they pretend it never crossed their minds. Fred has a great sense of timing. He throws himself over on his back and starts wagging his tail like a madman. This is his sign that he wants his belly rubbed, so I bend down and give his underside a good massage. He acts like a cat again. Usually I say a lot of goofy things to him when I rub him like this, but I don't do it in front of these people. I used to do it in front of Grandmother. She used to do it too. Fred relaxed her a lot. I look around her living room now and think that there probably isn't anyone else in the room except maybe my cousin, the warm kisser, who would have even thought of rubbing Fred's belly. Uncle Bert, Aunt Louise's husband, was petrified about a million years ago. I smile at Julia a little bit, and she smiles back. She's OK, I guess.

"That's good," I continue, "that you're not worried. I thought that maybe I could stay on here."

They all look at me as though I had taken a shot at them.

"It's my house now, isn't it? I'd like to take care of it. Grandmother would want it taken care of."

Mother laughs. She's always laughing. She has a big laugh. It's fake. It's a cover for the fact that she wants to say something sarcastic—not that she's shy about being sarcastic. She laughs a lot when she's being sarcastic too.

"Of course it's your house now, Davy," Aunt Louise says, "but you can't live in it."

"Why not?"

"You're only a boy. Boys don't live in houses by themselves."

"Fred will be here with me."

Now everyone laughs, and I half laugh. Maybe they buy that, the business about Fred being here. A dog is good protection, and maybe they're worried that I would get hurt or robbed or something like that.

"Among other things, we'd be arrested for leaving a minor alone in a house like this," Aunt Louise says. "But that's not the real problem. It's you we're thinking of, Davy. Without Mother, you can't live here alone. Who would cook your meals, and take care of you when you were sick, and see that you did your homework and went to school?"

It would be great to be in the house alone with Fred. I wouldn't mess things up. I'd leave everything the way Grandmother wanted it—except that she doesn't care anymore. I guess I'd make a few changes. I'd take down the curtains. That would be the first thing. And I'd throw away a lot of dishes, especially the ones with the flowers on them.

"David," Uncle Bert croaks, "your aunt and I would like you to come and live with us. We'd be pleased to have you in our home. You'd be welcome."

Aunt Louise looks at me anxiously, then at Mother. Uncle Jess looks at the floor very hard. My great-aunt is still looking ossified, but Cousin Julia is smiling in an encouraging way.

"Of course, if you'd like to come to Los Angeles," Uncle Jess stammers, "there will always be room for you with me, Davy. Would you like that?"

That really kills me. Me in California! Uncle Jess looks nervous, as though I might take him up on his invitation.

"I don't know," I finally say. "I really like it here."

Aunt Louise looks cheery, and I look at Mother. She has been smoking cigarettes as if they were going to be outlawed tomorrow and not saying a word. One cigarette is half-finished in the ashtray in front of her, and she is smoking another.

"What do you think, Mother?" I ask.

Everyone turns to Mother, who begins to look like an experiment in a chemistry laboratory. She keeps changing color, from pale white to flush pink and back, and the smoke is pouring out of her mouth and her nose almost at the same time. She takes a big drag on one cigarette and then lights another from it. "You're getting so many offers of bed and board that I really feel ashamed. You belong with me, David. I am your mother. These other people, they all love you, but it is you and I who are closest. Of course you will come to New York to live with me. I won't hear of anything else." She squashes out her cigarette in the ashtray. This one isn't even one-quarter gone.

Fred whimpers a little bit.

"I guess he wants some water," I say. I go out to the kitchen. Fred follows along. I toss out his stale water and fill up his bowl again. As soon as the tap is running, there is noise from the living room, but I don't want to hear it, so I turn the water higher and start singing to myself. Not just to me, but to Fred too. I'm not singing anything special. Sort of a combination of "The Star-Spangled Banner" and "Onward Christian Soldiers," but faster and more up-to-date than they usually sound. I'm a regular hummer when it comes to musical talent, but sometimes even hummers have to sing a song or two. I turn the faucet on and off frantically—on one second, off the next; on one second, off the next—and I'm shouting away so they can all hear: "Onward Christian soldiers, on to victory...on to victory."

five

My great-aunt and Cousin Julia leave late in the afternoon. Everyone is kissing everyone else. My great-aunt is the last living person in the family who is about Grandmother's age, so she probably figures that the next time we all get together it will be for her. I feel sorry for her on account of that, so I kind of kid around with her.

"I'll come to live with you, if you want me to, Auntie," I tell her.

Auntie almost croaks right there in front of me when I tell her that.

"I'm kidding," I say.

Auntie still looks like she's croaking.

"How about you and me?" I say to smoochy Julia. Julia thinks that's great and gives me one of her warm hugs. Honest to God, she ought to go into the circus as Miss Lovable or something like that.

Mother and Uncle Jess are staying in the house with me. There are four bedrooms. Grandmother's is up front, right over the porch. You can sit in the window up there and look at everything going on up and down the street. When I was a little kid and had to stay home because I was sick, I used to drag my own chair up to Grandmother's window and enjoy myself for an hour or two every afternoon. I find that I get a lot out of staring at people, just to see the way they walk, for example. Some women in particular walk like their feet hurt, but if you look at them a long time, from down the street to when they pass out of sight, you can imagine that it isn't their feet. It's some terrible thing at home. They don't have enough money to buy meat for supper, or their kid plays hooky all the time. When men walk down the street, they don't show you as much about themselves as women do. I think women are more obvious than men. That's just one thought I have had while sitting at Grandmother's window, which of course I still do from time to time. It makes me a little scared to think that I may not sit there too many more times. I even think maybe I'll move into her room tonight, because it's my house now, so I might as well live in the room where you can see everything. But I decide that I'd better not. I'll stay in my own room. Mother and Uncle Jess are sleeping in the small bedrooms. I guess it will be uncomfortable for whoever is the first one to sleep in Grandmother's bed, where she died, even though I think she wouldn't have minded. She was only sick for a few hours anyway. When you have a heart attack, sometimes they can't even get you to the hospital.

After my great-aunt and Julia have gone, Aunt Louise says that we'll all go over to her house for supper. Mother says No, and they have a big dumb argument about who's going to make the supper and who's going where to eat it. They begin to yell at each other, so Fred starts to bark. Both Mother and Aunt Louise scream "Shut up!" at Fred, who runs over to hide behind my legs. I don't blame him. The ladies themselves are surprised at their vehemence, so Uncle Jess steps in to save the day.

"I'll go buy Chinese and bring it back," he offers. "How's that?"

Everyone thinks that's a great idea, especially me. Grandmother hated Chinese food, but I like it, so this will be a big treat. Uncle Jess piles me and Fred into Uncle Bert's car, and we zip off to the Chinese restaurant to buy supper. While we're waiting for the meal in the restaurant, Fred is yelping away out in the car. Uncle Jess and I take turns going out there to shut him up, which is impossible. On one of Uncle Jess's trips out he stops in the liquor store next to the restaurant. He puts about four bottles into the car with Fred, who has a great time ripping the paper bag to pieces. At least he is quiet until the restaurant cashier has our cartons ready for us. We zip back to the house, where Mother and Aunt Louise are at fever pitch once again.

"They're arguing about dessert now," Uncle Jess says.

We both kind of laugh. He's OK, I guess.

Since they shut up like clams when we open the door, I

figure out right away that they've been at it about me again. When people try to hide things from you, they shouldn't be nice to you. They ought to ignore you or throw a pie at you or do something other than smile.

I'm carrying the Chinese food, and Uncle Jess has the bottles. Mother jumps up when she sees Uncle Jess.

"You're a darling!" she says in this phony way. She takes the bottles to the kitchen, and the next thing I hear is the refrigerator door opening and ice cubes being popped into glasses.

No one pays attention to the food, so I bring it to the kitchen too. I'm not even out of the room before Aunt Louise says, "Jess, how could you?"

"What do you mean, how could I? I want a drink."

"But, Jess," Aunt Louise continues, "you know..." She never finishes the sentence.

Mother is bustling around the kitchen. She gives me a big smile, a really friendly one, and I think that she can be a pretty attractive woman when she puts her mind to it.

"What do you have there, darling?" She kind of coos at me.

"Supper," I answer.

"Of course, dear. Put it over there." She points to the stove. "We'll warm it up in a few minutes." She pokes her head into the living room and sings away, "Scotch or bourbon, friends?" They all say something in answer and Mother comes back to the glasses.

"Very weak, Helen," Aunt Louise calls. "A lot of water."

"Yes, dear," Mother answers. She fills all of them about

halfway to the top and pours in tap water. She sees me standing there. "Nothing for you. Not this year, precious." Everyone is darling and dear and precious, and I'm ready to konk her over the head with the chow mein if she doesn't shut up. Fred is smelling the food and sitting there on his hind legs, begging for a taste. I stoop down and play around with him for a while. Mother sails off into the living room with the drinks, so I lie on my back and let Fred give my face one of his famous lick jobs since it doesn't look as though any of us is going to have a taste of the Chinese in the next ten minutes.

Fred and I roll around on the floor for some time, and I must admit I'm getting a little hungry. I open one of the cartons on top of the stove, and the food has already begun to look as though someone melted a layer of wax paper over it. I turn on the oven, which I always liked to do for Grandmother. It's a gas oven, and she used to say she got nervous holding the match to the little hole you stick it into, so wouldn't I do it for her. To tell the truth, I know she didn't get nervous about this particular thing. She just knew that I liked to hear it go pop when it caught, so she always had me do it. Then one day I read somewhere in a paper or a magazine that the thing to do with a match after you had used it was stick it in water just to make sure it was out before you threw it in the trash, and I told her about this. She said Yes, that was a good idea and she'd try to remember to do it. I somehow got it in my mind that she wouldn't remember and that if I weren't there to irrigate her used matches her house would catch fire. She let me be responsible for a lot of things like that, or she let me *feel* responsible anyway.

Mother comes in from the living room, followed closely by Aunt Louise.

"One is all Bert and I take, Helen," my aunt says.

"Don't be silly, darling." Mother has all the glasses and is popping ice cubes into them so fast that Aunt Louise has a new drink in her hand before she knows what has happened. Mother glides over to the stove and dips her finger into the opened carton.

"Yummy!" she says, then kisses me on the forehead. "It's yummy, darling. We'll put it together in a few minutes." She takes my hand and more or less pulls me into the living room. She steps on Fred's tail, and he yelps.

"That's what you get for being so long," she says to Fred. I can see that Mother and Fred are having the love affair of the century.

We're all sitting around in the living room. Fred has jumped into my lap and is fast asleep, and Uncle Jess is telling Uncle Bert about a modeling assignment he had in Ibiza two months ago. Uncle Bert says he would like to go to Ibiza, and Mother interrupts with a sort of shriek. "Bert! You in Ibiza! It's too funny!" She laughs very loud. Aunt Louise and Uncle Bert look angry.

"Why not Ibiza?" asks Aunt Louise.

"Bert is not exactly an international island-hopper, darling," Mother answers. "Can't you see Bert in Ibiza?" she asks Uncle Jess, who looks embarrassed.

"I'd like to know what seems so funny to you about Bert in Ibiza," Aunt Louise says. She is boiling mad.

"If you'd said Nantucket, that I could have understood," Mother says. "But Ibiza! Come on, darling."

Aunt Louise jumps up. "I'll go warm up the supper. We're all starving." She runs out to the kitchen, and I can hear a lot of dishes being rattled around.

"Let me help, darling," Mother calls out. There is no answer, and Mother doesn't move, so we all sit waiting for Aunt Louise to bring in the Chinese. Mother finishes her drink. "I mean it, darling," she calls again, getting up. "Let me help." She goes out to the kitchen, and they have a few words with each other before Aunt Louise brings in the supper. Mother helps her. She gives Uncle Jess and me plates, and we all sit down to eat. Mother has a new drink.

"Well, my dear," Mother says to me. "It's all settled. Right?" I think I know what she's saying, but I don't know how to answer her. "You want to come to live with your momma, don't you?"

I've only eaten a couple of mouthfuls of my supper, but I'm not as hungry as I thought.

"New York is the greatest city in the world for kids. There is absolutely no other place like it in the world. There's more of everything there. Got it? More of everything. Whatever you want, New York's got it. You agree with me, don't you, Jess?"

Uncle Jess looks at his food. "It's a great city, of course," he says. "It's nothing like Boston."

"What did I tell you?" Mother says. "So it's all settled. Right?"

I don't know if I'm supposed to answer or not. Is she asking me or telling me? No one helps me. Everyone is looking the other way as though I were a criminal or had done something wrong.

"Well…" I try to say something. "I don't know, Mother. It's like I said. I like it here. This is my home."

"A kid's home is with his mother," she says.

"Sure. All the kids have got parents."

Mother looks at me very quickly when I say that, and not in a friendly way.

"And all the kids live with their parents, right?" she says.

"Sure."

"So what's the big discussion about? You come live with me. I'll find you a good school, and your father will put you in it. OK?"

I look dumb, I guess.

"We'll have a time! There are places in New York I have wanted to see for twenty years! What a time it will be, seeing them together!" She begins to sound as though she really wants me, and I must admit that for the first time it seems remotely feasible.

"I don't know…" I blurt out.

"What's there to know? You're coming! In a few weeks! I'll make a few changes in the apartment, and then you'll come! OK, sweetheart?" She sounds so enthusiastic now that I'm sure it will work out fine.

"Well, I guess it will be OK," I say, "if it's OK with

everyone else." They all keep looking away. Aunt Louise sighs deeply. Hardly anyone has touched his Chinese. Fred woke up a minute ago and is going crazy trying to get within licking distance of a plate. "What about Fred?" I ask.

"I'm sorry, dear," Mother says. "You'll have to give Fred away."

"No!" I say. Everyone looks surprised. "I wouldn't give Fred away!"

"But, sweetheart," Mother says, "it's only a little apartment. I mean, just squeezing in one more person—" She stops before she can finish her thought.

"I don't care if you squeeze me in or not," I say. I'm yelling. "I don't care what you do. Any of you. None of you matter to me anyway. None of you really loved Grandmother like Fred and me. Grandmother wouldn't have let anyone split us up."

"Of course she wouldn't, dear," Mother says, "but that doesn't have anything to do with bringing Fred to New York. Mother would never have wanted Fred to come some place where there wasn't room for him."

"If there isn't room for Fred, there isn't room for me!" I say. I get up. "Excuse me," I say. I go to my bedroom. Fred follows and jumps on my bed when I throw myself on it. He whines a little bit, the bright bastard. He knows what has happened. I guess I cry for a couple of minutes. Fred stops whining and licks away the tears rolling down my cheeks.

six

For the next couple of days Aunt Louise is in and out, and she and Mother are having a great time screaming at each other about everything they talk about. I'm telling you, the decibel count went up about six hundred percent on our street by the end of the weekend. The principal thing they argue about is the house and what should be done about it. Should it be sold or rented? If it's sold, it will take so long to settle Grandmother's estate, but if it's rented, there will be income for me, and I'll be able to go to college. But I'll be able to go to college anyway, if it's sold and the money is invested. Real brilliant arguments, you can see.

The second thing they argue about is chairs, which belonged to their grandmothers and great-grandmothers and a variety of other ancestors—and things like handmade bedspreads, some of those funny dishes with flowers painted all over them, and a whole lot of other junk. The argument about the big clock is the funniest. That argument lasts off and on for about six days. It's one of those clocks made two hundred years ago. It weighs a ton and a half, I guess, and there's a lot of stuff carved all over it and a pretty good picture of a ship on it. To tell the truth, without thinking much about it, I always liked that clock. This particular argument is settled by Uncle Jess.

"It's the only thing I want from the house," he says. Since there's no topping that, Uncle Jess is awarded the clock. Of course, he doesn't get the last word on it.

"You'll have to pay the shipping charges to Los Angeles," Mother says. She's a real gracious loser.

They're always arguing about me too, but I don't get the gist of those arguments because they make elaborate efforts not to have them when I'm around. When I get tired of hearing the discussions about the house and the furniture, I figure they're tired of them too and would like to change the topics of disagreement. So I take Fred for walks a lot during these days. He's delighted of course. It isn't too often that he is taken out about ten times a day. He gets out so often now that sometimes when we come in again he looks at me as though he's apologizing for not having done his business outside. I tell him that's OK, he doesn't have to do his business ten times a day, three are enough. Mother keeps saying I'm nuts to talk to him in sentences, that all he understands are short, one-word commands, and that people like me who talk to animals have personality defects. She's all heart.

One of our walks is a long one, on Saturday. Grandmother has been buried for four days, and no one says anything much about her. In fact, it's almost as though they forgot why they're all together. She's been dead for a week. Last Saturday she made me a great breakfast—pancakes from some mix a buddy of hers brought back from Vermont, with some syrup that tasted as though it had just oozed out of a maple tree. That afternoon she had this heart attack, and she died that night. I figure that since no one is going to talk about Grandmother, to me anyway, I'd better take a walk over to where she is buried just to be sure everything is all right. The cemetery is not too far from the house, maybe two miles. It's in a part of the town where a lot of Italian people live. Whenever I meet an Italian kid, I always figure he lives near the cemetery. That's crazy of course, because Italian kids live everywhere. It just goes to show you what nutty ideas people get into their heads. I figure that since the cemetery is filled with gravestones and I have seen all these great pictures of Rome and Italy with stone pillars and a lot of marble, it is natural that Italians would live around cemeteries where they would feel closer to their heritage than in any other part of the town. I'm great on ethnic origins.

I put a leash on Fred for a long walk like this one. When he's just going out around the house or to the beach near the house, I figure that Fred doesn't need a leash. He obeys me very well when we're outside. But I don't walk to the cemetery part of town too much, so it's better that Fred knows who's boss right from the beginning on this particular stroll.

He hates the leash. But he likes to go to new places, which gives him a chance to sniff at a thousand new spots on the sidewalk, curbstones, corners of walls, fire hydrants, and trees. Old long Fred. When that doggie sniffs, all of him sniffs. He starts with his nose naturally, but in a second his chest is heaving in and out, his rear is moving, and his tail is wagging. He accepts the leash as the price of having all those marvelous new sniffs.

We get to the cemetery in about an hour. Fred has sniffed a lot, but not so much that we couldn't get anywhere. I find where Grandmother is buried, in the old part of the cemetery in a large grassy plot. I look at the gravestone and see that my grandfather died nineteen years before Grandmother.

There are a lot of wilted flowers piled up. Fred goes crazy. The flowers don't smell like flowers but have sort of a putrid smell. Fred loves them. He throws himself into the pile, runs his head and neck over the profusion of color, and generally enjoys himself, which makes all the money tied up in those flowers seem worthwhile to me.

"Hey, Fred," I say, "this is where Grandmother is buried."

Fred looks at me, but he doesn't stop rubbing around.

I think that maybe Grandmother would like him to do this.

"You don't mind, do you, Grandmother?" I hear myself asking aloud. It is quiet in the cemetery, with the exception of the noise Fred makes on the flowers.

"They're going to sell the house or rent it," I can't stop

myself from saying. "Mother wants me to go to New York to live with her. I think she wants me. Do you think she wants me?"

I don't know what I think is going to happen, but I wait for an answer.

"She doesn't want Fred. I won't go without Fred. I didn't mind going to visit her for a weekend without Fred because Fred was with you. Now he can't be with you any more. I thought maybe Fred and I could stay in the house alone, but no one will let me."

Fred has stopped rubbing around now, and he looks at me as though I'm crazy. I sit down on the flowers with him. I hold him in my arms, which is all he needs to fall asleep in two seconds.

"What do I do now?"

I lie back on the flowers. One bunch has a blue ribbon on it, with crummy-looking gold letters reading "Love Davy." I pick off the letters.

"That was a good breakfast, Grandmother," I say. "I didn't tell you last Saturday, but it was. You're a very good cook. I always wanted to tell you. And Fred liked the way you cooked too. Didn't you, Fred?"

I guess I am the world's number-one crybaby this week, because I start bawling again. Fred wakes up and licks my tears, and I say a lot of crazy things to Grandmother, like how I'll never forget her, and when I'm as old as Mother and Aunt Louise I won't be arguing all the time, and please, God, keep Grandmother warm this winter and forever.

I finally drag myself off the flowers. I put the crummy

gold letters in my pocket along with two wilted flowers. Fred and I go home.

"You've been for a long walk, sweetheart, haven't you?" Mother says when we come in. She is sitting there with Uncle Jess. They are having drinks.

"Yes," I answer.

"Where did you go?" Mother asks.

"Oh, no place."

"You must have gone some place!"

"Just around."

"Be that way," she says. "We've been thinking." She nods to Uncle Jess. "If Fred means so very much to you, sweetheart, he should come to New York too. What would you think of that?"

Think of it! I stand there like a twirp for a minute, and then I guess my mouth spreads from one ear to the other.

"You mean it?" I ask.

"Sure," she says.

I run over to her and give her a big kiss. I think she gets a little embarrassed, because our kisses have usually been more or less formal. But she carries it off OK.

"You've got to promise to do all the work though," she says. "I'll just have the fun."

seven

They let me make the final decision on Grandmother's house. I decide to rent it. After my mind is made up, I'll say this for Mother and Aunt Louise—they take to consulting me about a lot of things they hadn't before. They ask me what I think about leaving some of the furniture in the house so it can be rented furnished, and what I think about how much we should charge, and when I will be ready to let people see it. They must have read a book on child psychology. After two weeks of whispering about me and arguing with each other, they suddenly start consulting me about things, and I'll admit that I feel better disposed to the whole big deal. We find a tenant in another week, a guy who wants to move his wife and little kid in before Christmas, who will take the house for two years. When Fred throws himself on his back in front of the guy and the guy rubs his belly like he is supposed to, I figure he will be a good person to be a landlord to.

Mother is very perky after the business about the house is settled, and when we sign the lease she insists we give a big party for Mr. Henderson, the tenant. For Mother, giving a big party means having a large number of drinks, so Aunt Louise pooh-poohs that right away, but Mother won't let Mr. Henderson out of the house until he agrees to have a highball with her. Mr. Henderson has one drink. As he's leaving he says he's looking forward to showing his wife the house and knows she'll love it because she likes old things.

"If there are problems about anything, just ask me," Mother urges. Since she plans to go back to New York in another few days, the offer isn't as generous as it seems. Mother tells me that she's done everything she can, don't I think? I tell her sure she has. To forestall one of the long talks she has been having with me in the last week when there's been no one else around, I tell her that I have a lot of homework to do. That's not a good reason for not talking "heart-to-heart" as Mother puts it, so I sit down and Mother talks. She tells me about all the plans she had for herself when she was a young girl, how fantastically popular she was in college, how she moved right along when she went to New York, how one bad mistake has set her back so that she has really had a whole decade robbed from her by my father, how difficult it was to get back into the swing of things when you had given everything you had to your family, how now she was a happy and mature adult and was looking forward to having a wonderful life with me, and so on. I say Yes and No when she wants me to, and an hour and a half later she tells me that we've had a good talk, haven't we? I tell her we have, and she tells me I stay up too late for my age. So I take Fred out for his finals and tumble into bed, knowing that in another week or so I'll not be sleeping here again.

Mother goes back to New York a few days later. Fred and I move in with Aunt Louise temporarily. Mother will get her apartment ready for us in a few weeks, so I can move down during Christmas vacation. I'm so busy shuffling myself around now that the time goes by fast. I tell Mother I want to bring a lot of stuff to New York, and she tells me I can bring about a quarter of it. She sends me the measurements of my closet and tells me that in New York everything has got to be shoved into little spaces and that every inch will be important. I can't bring my own bed and my own chest. They are too big. She is talking with a decorator about my room, and it's going to be lovely. I say good-bye to a lot of people, everyone in school and all the teachers. I'm planning to visit Aunt Louise in the summer, so it's not as though I'm not going to see all these people again. I tell about thirty guys that they can visit me in New York, and I wonder what Mother will think about that. I kiss Mary Lou Gerrity good-bye. It's not the first time I've kissed her, but it's the first time we've opened our mouths when we kissed. Mary Lou tells me afterwards that she will be faithful to me, and I tell her that I will be faithful to her too, though I really had no intention of getting that involved. She said it first, so there was nothing else I could do.

I take Fred to the cemetery a lot now, almost every day. Aunt Louise's house is even closer than Grandmother's. I begin to feel guilty on days when I don't go to visit. When I come the next day, I always tell Grandmother that I'm sorry I wasn't there yesterday. I tell her about everything that has happened during the day and about all the plans for New York. I ask her if that's OK with her. I guess I cry a lot. I don't want to leave her behind. It's cold now, and I know it's very cold underground, and when there isn't anyone to come to talk with you, the cold is worse, I am sure. Can you hear me, Grandmother? Will you know when I'm not coming any more that it's not because I don't love you? It's because I'm in New York. Fred always lifts his leg on the gravestone.

eight

I'd never visited Mother in her new apartment, which I hadn't realized was in an old house on a street that looks like New York must have looked a hundred years ago. Now I know what they mean by blocks. Before, when Mother told me such and such a friend lived two blocks away from her and they didn't visit each other at night unless they had escorts, I thought maybe a block was, say, ten miles. It isn't. It can be twenty skinny houses' worth and take only two minutes to walk. Where Mother lives, some blocks look OK to walk on, but others look as though you might want to walk around them. That's why Mother and her buddy don't visit, I guess.

Aunt Louise and Uncle Bert had decided to pile me and Fred into their Chrysler and take us and our stuff to Mother's the day after Christmas. Everyone had agreed that this was the sensible thing to do. We would avoid train tickets and a lot of Railway Express charges for my stuff, and we would get Fred to New York with the least amount of noise from him. Fred loves cars, and nothing makes him happier than to take a long drive.

Mother's house is in the middle of the block. It was built in 1834 and has high ceilings. There are a couple of fireplaces in her apartment and a nutty-looking porch over the kitchen of the people who live under her on the second floor. We're all shivering with the cold when we come in, and it's the back porch Mother wants to show us first. She calls it her terrace, and I can see right away that she thinks Fred can live out there. I tell her that Fred loves heat, and if she will show me where I'll live, I'm sure Fred can squeeze in there too. She's very real-estate agent about the whole thing though, so we have to wait to see my room. We see her study, which has a desk in it with a quill pen stuck in a china inkwell. Then we see her bedroom and her bed, which is a sight, with a big floppy lace ceiling over it. We see the kitchen, which must have been a closet in former days, and the bathroom.

"It's for both of us," she says. She opens four doors and finally shows me a shelf she calls mine. "For your personals, darling," she says. "Shaving things and all that." She laughs. This makes me mad. Some of the guys at home have already had one or two shaves, but I haven't, and to tell the truth I'd like to. I haven't even had any hair to speak of under my arms yet, but I think I'm getting some. I understand that after that, it will come to my upper lip pretty fast. The thing is, L. T. Murray had hair under his arms as long ago as the fifth grade. He showed it to me a lot and told me that if I would rub spit in this area, hair would come very fast. L. T. didn't know what he was talking about of course, as I discovered.

We see Mother's living room, which is great. It has some big couches and funny-looking leather chairs. She has a fire going, and Fred has already curled himself up in front of it, at home in five minutes.

"Now the *pièce de résistance*!" Mother declares. She flings open a door off her living room, and there is my room. It's all boy, all right. She has had it paneled and has had some skinny drawers built in a skinny double-decker bed. She's got a strange collection of stuff on the walls, and she tells me they are from Childcraft. They're great of course, but they're for kids about five. She's also got a teddy bear sitting up on my pillow.

"You remember it, don't you, darling?" she says. "I've kept it always." I'm embarrassed because I don't remember it. "It was your first toy. You loved it so." She is sort of slobbering all over me. Aunt Louise and Uncle Bert look away, and I don't know what to do.

"Sure," I say. "I remember it. I wondered what happened to it."

"I knew you would!" Mother says. She looks at Aunt Louise. "It was an important influence in his earliest years. It is a security symbol. That's really why I kept it. I knew Davy would need it again." She grabs the teddy bear off the bed and gives it a big kiss. By this time Fred has seen it and is sitting up begging to play with it. Boy, could he make something of that security symbol in three minutes! I tell Fred to get down, and Mother tells all of us that she has the loveliest family in the world and everything is going to be so wonderful now that Davy and she are together and it's nice to have Fred living here too. They move back to the living room. I stay behind in my room for a minute. The mattress on my bed is OK, and it's pretty neat that Mother had another bed built on top of mine. Both of them are so narrow though, that I'm not sure I'd want to sleep in the top bunk. That will be for the people I invite, I guess. Fred is sniffing away at everything. He's having a marvelous time. I'm hoping he won't lift his leg on anything which happens to smell too delicious not to baptize. At least not tonight.

Mother says she's asked in one or two friends to meet me and that of course Aunt Louise and Uncle Bert will stay too. Aunt Louise says sure, and they go off in their Chrysler to find a hotel to live in for the night. Mother tells them to stay at the Chelsea. It's only a few blocks away, and she says it is fabulous. It's filled with writers and painters, and a man on the top floor keeps a lot of giant snakes in an apartment he has there. Aunt Louise's shoulders rise up to around her ears on that one, and she gives Mother her "Oh, Helen" look.

"Really, darling," Mother says, "it's absolutely marvey. It has rooms large enough to divide by six, and still there'd be space enough for everyone. It's where Dylan Thomas used to live when he was in New York. Arthur Miller stays there too. Thomas Wolfe lived there. If I were from someplace else, I'd want to stay there."

Uncle Bert asks if the Statler isn't nearby, and Mother gives him one of her laughs for people out of touch with the Chelsea Hotel. She says that what used to be the Statler is indeed nearby and they can get a room there if they want to, but what is the point of being in New York if they stay in a hotel just like any old hotel they might find in Boston.

With Aunt Louise and Uncle Bert out hotel-hunting, Mother asks if she can't help me unpack. We open up my two suitcases and four cartons with all my junk in them. She's great, taking my stuff out of the suitcases. She says that I have good-looking suits, but how come I have only two? I tell her two suits are plenty, and she says that I'll have to get some more because this school she has got me enrolled in has a requirement about how people have to dress. She folds up all my shirts and my underwear so they will fit in the skinny drawers in the chest she got made for my room.

The funny thing about it is that she keeps telling me what she's doing. She says Oh, another shirt; this is a blue one; isn't it nice and fresh? Let's shake it out and fold it long and narrow. Oh, here's a lovely tattersall shirt; isn't that nice? Is that the one I gave you for Christmas? It hasn't been worn yet. And then she yells a little. I've stuck my finger on one of the pins, she says, and then she laughs and says What the hell, I'm not going to take out all the pins just to put it in your drawer. Here, she says, you take care of this one. Why haven't you worn it yet? I tell her that I just opened the Christmas box two days ago, and she says, Of course, and was I saving the shirt for later? I say Yes. She asks do I like it? Sure, I say. You mean that, sweetheart? Sure. You wouldn't put your mother on, would you? No, I say. Did you like it as well as anything you got for Christmas? Well, I say, I don't know. You gave me some other stuff too. She says that's right. What other things that she gave me did I like? I tell her I like the stopwatch I asked for and which she gave me. She says what do I need a stopwatch for? I tell her about my running and how I was probably the fastest runner in my class at home. And I tell her about the relay teams I have been captain of for the last three years and how they have won all the races for my age group ever since I've been the captain. She thinks that is wonderful.

"Have you really, darling?" she asks.

"Sure," I say.

"I didn't know an Olympic athlete would be moving in with me!" she says. But when she says it, I know it's phony. She doesn't care about the relay races in the same way Grandmother did. There's nothing I can put my finger on, but I think for a minute that my mother is getting a big laugh out of me. I guess relay races don't mean anything when you aren't running in them, but when you have been the captain of a winning team for three years, as I was, and when the team had a couple of fat guys on it who weren't good runners but who worked to be better runners than other fat guys and became pretty good runners anyway in spite of being fat, you don't want somebody to make fun of the team. When I was living with Grandmother, she used to come to all the track meets I was in.

She always told me that it was better to be part of a winning team than to win all by myself. I think she was just trying to make me feel OK because I could never win the hundred-yard dash or the pole vault or anything like that. I got some second- and third-place ribbons for those things though. One year I won the high jump. Grandmother told me that she was glad I had jumped higher than anyone else, but she still thought that the relay-team win was more impressive. She took me to the movies that night. It was the first time I had gone at night. I remember that night very well, because in addition to going to the movies, we had an ice-cream soda afterwards, and it was almost eleven o'clock when we got home. Fred was waiting for us at the front door, and we took him right out for his finals, but when we came back and I went upstairs to my bedroom, I discovered that Fred had been in my bed and ripped up my sheets. He didn't like Grandmother and me to leave him behind while we celebrated. If there were any parties in his house, he wanted to be part of them. From then on when we had to be out at night, poor Fred was cooped up in the kitchen, which was OK I guess because it smelled of food and was always warm. It showed me that when you make a dog like Fred part of your family, he is a full-time member, not just someone who will be around when you want him to.

Mother and I get out about half of my stuff before her doorbell rings. That is all Fred needs. He really lets himself go when he hears the buzz. I knew he could bark, but I had never heard him wail before. I laugh.

"My God!" says Mother. "Can't you keep the little bastard quiet?" She goes to her doorbell button and presses it. I can hear the noise of the buzzer downstairs and the sound of the front door of the house opening. But these are only dim sounds, crowding out the pounding in my head. She has called Fred a little bastard. It wasn't her friendly voice. I have heard her call people bastards a lot before, but there was nothing to it. I call people bastards all the time, not to their faces but to myself. People are coming up the stairway. I want to grab Fred and run into my room, but Fred is standing at the living-room door, barking away.

"Stop it!" Mother yells at him.

Fred only barks louder.

"Davy." She turns to me. "You've got to stop him!"

I go to Fred. "Here, Fred," I say. He keeps barking at the footsteps coming up the stairs.

"My God, Fred," Mother yells, "will you shut up!"

I grab Fred and pull him away from Mother's door. He only barks louder as I carry him into my room. I pull him up onto my bed with me, holding a hand over his muzzle. He can't make noise then, but he is wiggling in my arms as Mother's friends come into her living room.

"Darling!" Mother says. "Davy's chaining down the welcoming committee in the other room!" She laughs her loud, hysterical laugh.

"That's fabulous, darling," a lady's voice says, laughing like Mother afterward.

"Really mad," says a man.

My door is partly open. The guests brush their cheeks

against Mother's. I do not want to go out to meet them. Fred is squirming wildly in my arms. I give him a big kiss. This makes Fred happy, and he has a fine, slurpy time licking my face.

nine

Mother's friends keep coming to her apartment for the next few days. The women always give Mother a big kiss, and Mother kisses them back, and they all call each other darling and things like that. All the men who come look like each other. When they say darling to Mother, they don't say it loud like the women. When I am introduced to them, they ask me how I am and am I enjoying New York and what grade am I in. I am glad that Fred does a lot of barking because that gives me a chance to talk about how much Fred barks and to explain that in our town it was very quiet, and that the people who came to visit our house were usually people like Aunt Louise and Uncle Bert or maybe some ladies who used to come to play bridge with my grandmother. Fred barked then too, but that was different. Then he had to protect his turf only once a week. Now he has to protect it several times a day.

Mother tells me that's the way it is during the holidays, and I can see that she is ready to clobber Fred. So I take him out for a lot of long walks. There's no question of letting him off his leash now. My walks are around the blocks near Mother's. When she has a lot of people visiting her, I walk around her blocks two or three times. I think that I'll get Fred tired out and he'll go to sleep when he goes up to Mother's apartment. He never does. He jumps all over Mother's friends and barks at every new one who comes.

Fred also has a very hard time learning where it is all right to do his business. Before, if Fred made a mess on someone's front lawn or right in front of someone's front door, it wasn't a big catastrophe. I used to push it into the street, and there weren't any hard feelings. Not in New York. The block Mother lives on is all fixed up, like Mother's place, to look like it looked a hundred years ago. It's very pretty compared to other blocks I can see from walking Fred in the neighborhood. The trouble is that everyone on the block knows it's very pretty. They spend a lot of time yelling at me not to let Fred plop in front of their houses. Fred doesn't understand what the yelling is about, and after three days he takes a raised voice as his cue to evacuate. This is no way to make friends in a new neighborhood. I decide that the problem is not one I want to have a "heart-to-heart" with Mother about. There's no one I can talk to about it. So I tell Fred what I guess are the rules of the game here in New York. Fred, gentleman that he is, is a good listener to my three-times-a-day lecture. I guess he thinks it's lovemaking. I can see right away though that we've got a big problem on our hands.

The fourth day I am at Mother's place sees Mother gloomier than usual at breakfast when Fred comes loping up to her chair and curls himself around her feet. She is wearing a bathrobe with light feathers around the bottom, and Fred enjoys nibbling at the hem. Mother keeps pulling it away from Fred. He thinks that's a big game, until finally she says, "This is a Christmas present, Davy! I'm not ready to turn the whole house over to Fred yet!"

I say I'm sorry. Fred likes the feathers. They tickle him, and when she moves them away from him, he doesn't understand that she isn't playing with him. He thinks that if he likes feathers, feathers are his friends.

"How do you know what he thinks?" Mother asks. "Dogs don't think. They just sit around and respond to every temptation they are faced with. I don't know why Mother ever got you Fred in the first place. We never had dogs when we were growing up."

"Grandmother loved Fred too."

"Oh, yeah?" Mother says in a loud voice. Then she stops saying anything at all and speaks softly. "Sure she did, Davy. I'm sorry, sweetheart. I shouldn't be angry with Fred. I'm not used to him yet."

She gets up from the table and puts her arm around me. "Give me a kiss."

She bends down, and I sort of kiss her. She laughs, friendly, as she *can* be when she wants to be. She bends down to rub Fred, who has been jumping all over her while she was kissing me.

"Oh, that's my Fred," she says, talking goofy. "Fred, Fred, Fred. That's a good doggie."

Fred is wagging his tail like some machine. He has decided that Mother is some big love of his life now. If he only knew what she was saying about him two minutes ago! She goes out to the kitchen to get more coffee for herself, and Fred follows her like she's Cleopatra. I can hear her making a few more goofy sounds at Fred in the kitchen. I'm pleased, I guess. But why did she say those things just a few minutes ago? I can't figure it out, and maybe I won't ever. So why bother? I pick up my plate, which is clean because I like scrambled eggs the way my mother makes them. She puts in cheese and onions and a whole lot of stuff so that they don't taste like eggs at all. The first day she did that, I let Fred lick the plate, but she said that was obscene. When I looked up the word in the dictionary, I decided that I wouldn't let Fred do that any more. Anyway, I pile a few other plates on my own to take them to the kitchen where Mother and Fred are making all that love, and I look into this mirror hanging on the wall. It's hung so that I can see out into the kitchen. I'm not looking into the mirror for any special reason, but I just happen to glance into it as I am bringing the dishes to the kitchen. I see Mother's reflection. She has this bottle of whiskey in her hands. Her eyes are closed, and I can see that she has just had a big swallow of it. I shiver, I guess. It's dumb, but I don't want her to know I have seen her in the mirror. Or I don't want her to know I have seen her at all is more to the point. I can't look away from the mirror. I want to turn away, but I want to know if she's going to have another drink out of the bottle. She raises it to her mouth and takes a big gulp. She's still talking to Fred too, and I get the impression that she's talking to Fred so friendly so that I will think what I thought, that there is some big love feast going on over the pot of coffee. She puts the bottle down with all the other bottles on her shelf and then pours coffee into her cup. I edge toward the kitchen with my plates.

"Hi," I say as though we just saw each other for the first time today.

"Hi, darling!" she answers. "Fred and I are going to run away to celebrate the New Year together! What would you think about that? Would you be jealous, sweetheart?" She gives me one of her big hugs.

"Come on," I say. "I'm going to break your dishes if you hug me." She smells like she does when she kisses me good-night.

She takes the dishes from my hands and puts them into her metal sink. "Dishes, dishes, dishes," she says. "What are dishes?"

Fred is sitting up on his hind legs now, begging for who knows what.

"Fred wants you to hug him," I say.

Mother makes the nutty noises people make to dogs when they guess they are talking to them. It's not exactly goochy-goo, but close to it. She does bend down to Fred and lets him give her a few big licks. I'm the real stiff in the picture, I conclude. So what if Mother wants whiskey in the morning? It's none of my business. Fred likes to give her licks regardless of what she drinks. Fred probably has more sense than I have. Right? Who's to say?

I tell Mother that I'd better take Fred out for a walk. "Didn't you take him before breakfast?" she asks.

"Yes," I say.

"He doesn't have to go out twenty times a day, Davy."

"Sure. I know that."

"Then why are you forever running down the stairs with him?"

"I don't know. He likes it, I think," I answer. "He likes to go out and sniff around. You know."

"As a matter of fact, I don't know." She says this with her snotty voice, the one I hate the most.

"It's that it's new for him, Mother. He likes to sniff around. That's all. And I'm not going to be able to take him out so much next week when I'm in school."

"You always seem to be going out or coming in with Fred, Davy. Aren't you two ever just going to stay?" Mother's voice cracks a bit when she says this, so I say sure we're going to stay. She understands that this is a new place for both of us, right? Maybe it takes us a little time to go out and come in at the right time, but we'll learn. Is that OK?

She says sure it's OK, and she's sorry that she sounds like a nag, and one of the biggest and most important things in her life is that she shouldn't sound like a nag, and more important that she shouldn't be a nag, and do I understand the difference?

I say sure I understand the difference. And I hope I didn't make her feel that I thought she was a nag. If I did, I'm sorry.

"Oh, no!" she says. "Davy, sweetheart, there's nothing to be sorry about. Oh, sweetheart, Mother wants most of all to have a lovely home for her baby. You understand that, don't you?"

I tell her sure I do. She gives me another one of her hugs, and I'm sorry, I want to get out of it. My stomach turns over inside, I think, and I pull away from Mother. Does she know it!

"There's something wrong with you animal lovers," she says very loud. "You think you're better than the rest of us. I'll tell you something, Davy sweetheart, animals are from hunger! Don't forget it!"

I look at Mother for a minute. She's nuts, I guess. I want to go back to my real home. I want this to be a short vacation, over on New Year's Day.

"I'm going to take Fred out," I say abruptly. "Come on, Fred." Fred's ready to go in half a second. I get my coat and go to Mother's front door.

"Take your damned dog out," she says. "Have yourself a damned good time. Stay out the whole damned day if you wish. Forget about your damned mother, Davy!"

I open the door and Fred races out into Mother's hallway. I run after him and the door slams shut. Oh, God, I think to myself.

"Oh, God," I hear Mother saying on the other side of the door.

ten

Two days later is the day before New Year's, and it's been arranged that my father will pick me up in the morning and we'll spend the day together. The doorbell rings around eleven, and Fred, old symphony orchestra that he is, howls a greeting to my father. My mother works the buzzer to let him in, and as he comes up the stairway Fred is crazier than ever. For the first time, Mother doesn't go berserk. I can see from the smile on her face that she's glad Fred is giving hell to my father. I don't anticipate that this will be a very cheery meeting, so I get out my overcoat, ready to put it on in half a second.

"Happy New Year, David," Mother says to my father after she has let him in.

Father tells her the same thing and then gives me a sort of kiss, not really a kiss, but he puts his arms around me and puts his face next to mine. I guess I'm awkward and don't know what to do.

"Hi," I say.

He says hi too and tells me Happy New Year as well. Fred is screaming at his heels, so he bends down in a second and Fred licks his hand.

"Hi, Fred," my father says. I'm pleased that he calls Fred by his name and my face shows it. My father says, "Fred and I are old friends, aren't we, Fred? You remember, Davy, I met Fred at your grandmother's."

"Oh, sure," I say. I remember that was one of the times I left Fred alone with Grandmother for a week, when my father took me on a trip. Grandmother told me that Fred wouldn't eat for two days after I went away. I don't think I was very hungry either.

No one says anything, so I say, "Do you want to see my room?"

Sure, he says, so Mother and I take him into my room. Mother is beaming with pleasure that I asked him, I guess, because she puts her arm on my shoulder as though we are buddies.

"Do you like it?" she asks.

"It's very nice," he answers.

"Look at the paneling, David," she says, running her hands up and down over the wall. "It's supposed to look like it came from an old barn. What do you think of it?"

"It's nice, very nice," my father says again.

"It's not from a real barn of course. It's synthetic. You could never tell the difference, could you?"

"No, I suppose not."

"What do you mean, suppose? You couldn't tell the difference in a million years unless you were a farmer. The decorator says it's actually better to use simulated paneling. Real barn paneling may deteriorate. Especially in the city. Davy likes it," she says. "Don't you, sweetheart?"

"Yes," I answer.

"See, David," Mother says. "It doesn't make any difference to Davy if it's real or synthetic." Then she sort of laughs. "When the bill comes, you'll see what a big savings it was to use fake." Mother opens the drawers where my clothes are. "Look, David," she says. "These are the drawers."

"I see," Father says.

"Don't you think it's marvelous the way they have been sort of worked in underneath things? Look," she says, tugging open another drawer, one built in under the bed, "here's another drawer. Isn't it marvelous? I more or less designed everything myself. Look at the bed." She pushes at the top bunk, raising the mattress there and letting it fall back in place. "There's an extra bed so Davy can invite friends to stay the night. What do you think of that?"

"Very nice," Father says.

"You don't sound enthusiastic. Or are you just thinking of the bill?"

"No, no," Father says. "It's just that it doesn't look like a real room."

"What do you mean by that?"

"Only that it doesn't look like anyone lives in it."

My mother gets red in the face. "I didn't design it all by

myself. I used a decorator. He has top clients too, David. I just gave him my ideas. I don't see what you find wrong with that."

"It looks like an advertisement for a boy's room," my father says.

"Davy loves the room!" Mother says. "Don't you, sweetheart?"

"I think it's swell," I lie.

"There!" Mother yells. Then she says, "Honestly..." or something like that under her breath. She almost pushes Father out of the room, which is very easy to do. With three people in the room, if one moves, two others get pushed.

Mother calms down a little bit and asks Father if he doesn't want some coffee before we go.

"No, thank you, Helen."

"Or a New Year's drink perhaps, to fortify you for your day's adventure?"

"No," Father says. He helps me put on my overcoat. Fred is sure he is going out with me, but he isn't. We leave. Fred is jumping up against the door. I can hear Mother arranging the breakfast utensils in her sink. It's lucky that manufacturers have developed unbreakable kitchen stuff is all I can say.

"We'll meet Stephanie at one thirty and have lunch," my father says when we get to the street. "Is that all right with you?"

"Sure," I say. Stephanie is my father's new wife. Not new. They have been married three years. I met her one time before they were married. Father brought her to Boston for the weekend and told me he was going to get married again. I didn't like it much, but I was only ten at the time. I always hoped that my mother and father would get together again. I thought maybe if they both came to stay at Grandmother's they'd get back together, but Grandmother wouldn't ever let me ask them like that.

Now that I think of it, Grandmother looked forward to seeing my father more than my mother. When Father was coming, Grandmother would make a lot of cookies and some custards she said he particularly liked. He never stayed more than one or two nights at a time, but I could tell from the way they talked that they got along OK. They never talked about my mother, at least while I was with them. Grandmother was nice to Stephanie when Father brought her that first time. I must admit I wasn't nice at all. I said hello and all that, and I answered when anyone asked me anything, and I was polite when I was supposed to be, but any way you cut it I was snotty. Stephanie didn't mind, and that made me mad. If she had worked harder to win me over, I might have been friendlier.

The next time I saw her was at her wedding, which was in her uncle's apartment in New York. It wasn't a real wedding like the ones in churches at home. It was like a party, which takes a long time to get started. There were only two other kids there. They were Stephanie's nephews. All told, there weren't more than forty people at the wedding. Everyone had a lousy time.

Since they have been married, I have seen Stephanie several times, though she didn't come with Father when he took me on vacation trips. When my father came to Boston on business for a few days, he would bring her along, and we'd all have dinner. Grandmother usually came, and before you knew it, Grandmother and Stephanie were kissing each other. I started kissing Stephanie too. And to tell the truth, it wasn't such a bad thing to do. It was my own idea. When she came over with Father last July and gave Grandmother a big kiss, I said something like What about me? or some other such original thought, and she looked at me for what seemed to be three minutes and then gave me a big hug. She bawled for just a second after. I knew I liked her for sure when she said to my father, "I knew I'd screw this one up. Give me your handkerchief." She wiped her eyes and blew her nose very loud. We laughed. That night we went out for dinner and had a great time looking at fireworks being shot off over Marblehead Harbor from the place where we were eating. I haven't seen Stephanie since then.

"Is there anything you would like to do before lunch?" my father asks.

"Oh, I don't know. Just walk around, if that's OK."

"Sure," he says.

And we walk around. Before, when I came to New York, there had always been something planned. I went to Radio City Music Hall so often that I wondered if Mother wanted to be a Rockette. She kept asking me if I liked it. And I kept telling her that it was great. To tell the truth I hated it.

Father doesn't say anything about going to Radio City.

He doesn't say anything about going anyplace. So we just walk down the street. Several streets. We come to a small grassy plot filled with gravestones.

"This is the third Spanish-Jewish graveyard," Father says.

"Oh," I say.

"Spanish Jews were in America long before your ancestors were, and even before all of mine were."

"Oh," I say again.

I look in over the wall protecting the graveyard and say that it looks well-kept. He asks me if I want to see the two earlier Spanish-Jewish graveyards, and I don't say anything.

"They're both beautiful," Father says.

"Sure," I say, "if you want me to see them."

"I don't *want* you to see them, Davy," Father says. "I thought you might be interested in them."

"Well, I don't know. Should I be?" I ask.

"It depends on you, Davy. If you want to see them, I'll show them to you."

"That would be nice," I say because I don't have anything else to say.

Father is quiet now. He doesn't say anything, and neither do I. We walk along the street and turn from one block to the other. We stop in front of Theodore Roosevelt's house, and Father asks me if I want to go in. I say No, and he says we'll go in another time. Will Father and I be going into historic houses until I grow up? I ask myself. Yes, I answer.

"Stephanie is Jewish, Davy," Father says. "Did you know that?"

I say No, and he asks me if I know any Jews. I tell him sure I do, and then I tell him the names of a lot of kids I know who are Jewish.

Father says let's go to Central Park, and I say OK. He says this as though he wants me to see a lot of Jewish people in Central Park. We get into a taxi and go to Central Park. Father tells me in the taxi about Stephanie's father, how he came from Poland, where it wasn't certain if a Jew was Polish or Russian or German, and how Stephanie's father, and her mother too, and all of her aunts, and everyone else in the family came from Poland. Now they are living on Riverside Drive in New York, and a few of them live in New York suburbs like Scarsdale, and they are proud of being Jewish and so should we be proud of Jews. I say that I guess I am proud of Jews.

"Of course you are, Davy," Father says. He puts his arm on my shoulder. I am pleased he does that. I move toward him in the taxicab. He holds me closer to him, and I don't know what gets into me. I kiss my father. It is the first time I've done that since I knew what I was doing and had some control over what I did. He has kissed me before, like this morning when he came to get me at Mother's. But he has never really kissed me as though he wanted to. Not that I remember. He holds me for a minute, and then I guess we decide that men don't get gushy over each other like this, and he lets me go. We don't say anything else until we get to Central Park.

As soon as I get into the park I know that it was a mistake not to bring Fred. There's grass. And wide spaces where people can run for hundreds of yards and not bump into other people. In half a second I can tell that most of the dogs prancing around are dogs like Fred—they live in apartments and houses like Mother's. I feel guilty. Fred wants a place he can feel free. He wants to dig in the sand again and own streets in the same way he owned the street we lived on at home. Maybe Central Park is a place Fred can feel as he should. I decide right away that I will bring him here as soon as I have some extra money for a taxi.

Father and I walk around looking at all the people. It's not cold for the last day of the year. It's almost like spring in fact, and some people are sitting on the grass.

"Is it OK to sit down?" I ask my father.

"Sure."

I sit on the grass. The earth is hard from the winter weather, not comfortable. The grass is not green, but it isn't brown either.

"The grass is kind of gray, isn't it?" I say, looking up at my father.

He looks around for a few seconds. "Yes, it is," he says. "Do you enjoy sitting on the grass?"

What a dumb question! I don't say anything. In half a minute I stand up.

"It's all right to sit if you want to," my father says. "Go ahead."

"No, that's all right," I answer. If you're going to sit on the grass, you should be alone or the person you are with should sit with you. I decide that I don't know why I kissed my father in the taxicab. Anyone who will make such a big production about sitting on the grass doesn't get kisses from me. Fred, doggie, come sit with me in the park!

We come to this restaurant in the park, and Stephanie is waiting for us. She gives me a big smooch and says she hopes I will have a Happy New Year. I say the same thing to her. She starts asking about how I like New York now that I live here, and I tell her that it's fine, but I'll let her know more about it when I start school in a few days and begin to find my way around the city. We have a good lunch, and Stephanie chatters away all through it. She keeps smiling at my father and touching me when she talks to me about all the places I will enjoy learning about. She says that her favorite place when she was thirteen was the Museum of Natural History and would I like to go there after lunch? I say sure I would. And I mean it. Animals and all that stuff. I like zoos better because those animals are alive, but Stephanie says she doesn't like zoos so much because the animals are in cages and they don't have a chance to be themselves. People are always looking at them and feeding them Cracker Jacks and a whole lot of junk, and the animals aren't free and natural as they were intended to be. My father says that this is the only way city people can get to know anything about live animals, so he doesn't think it's so bad. Stephanie asks him how he would like to be put on display so that people could learn his habits. We get a laugh out of that one, except that I

eleven

The school Mother has picked for me to go to is right next to the Episcopal church that runs it. When she told me about it, I thought I wouldn't like to go to a church school, especially since I haven't been to church much, and certainly not to the Episcopal church. Mother says I might as well be an Episcopalian as anything, and if they have religious education, that will be good for my soul.

The first thing I'm surprised about is that I have to pass a lot of other schools to get to mine. There are plenty of schools right in the neighborhood, but Mother says they are public schools, and my father should have to pay to give me a good private-school education. I can see that Mother must be a lot of fun to work up a family budget with.

On the first day at the school I see the blazers all the other guys are wearing, and Mother buys three right there on the spot. This is more sport coats than I have ever had

don't really know any of my father's habits, so I don't get as big a laugh as they do.

We go to the Museum of Natural History, which isn't far from the restaurant. I like it a lot. It has some dinosaur bones hooked together with wire and stretching for hundreds of feet. There are a lot of pictures showing how the dinosaurs looked when they had skin on them, and I notice that the bone structure in the heads of the tiny dinosaurs looks a little bit like what I guess Fred's bone structure would look like if I could see it. The thought makes me shudder though, so I wander out of the dinosaur section. There's a lot of stuff about American Indians which is pretty interesting, and so are the stuffed American wild animals. Stephanie says she hates this part the most, and she won't look at stuffed animals. She decides to wait for us while we look at them. They are all fixed up so that they seem to be in places where they would be found naturally. In addition to all the bears, there are a lot of wolves and animals like that, including a friendly looking coyote. The descriptive card next to him says that coyotes become very tame and make attractive pets if they are caught young.

"Fred might like a coyote for a buddy," I say.

"Your mother wouldn't though," Father answers.

"No. I guess not."

I put my hand up to the glass in front of the coyote. "Hello," I say.

"He's stuffed, Davy."

"Sure, I know."

I put my face against the glass.

"Hello."

Father walks away.

"Hello, coyote," I say again. "What was your name?"

The coyote just looks at me.

"You must have had a name. You could have been a pet. Some Indian kid's pet. Were you?"

He doesn't move, but I won't take my eyes off him. There's no one else in the corridor with the stuffed animals now.

"Coyote," I say, "do you want to be petted?" Of course he just looks at me.

"Do you?"

I think he sees me. Honestly. There is something in his eyes which makes me believe that he understands that I am there and talking to him as a friend. I swear that he understands that I am his friend.

"Davy!" I hear my father calling me from far away. "I'm coming," I answer.

"Come on, Davy!"

I look again at the coyote.

"I'll be your friend. So will Fred. You'll have two friends in New York City."

He stares at me still, but there's more there than the blank stare he had before. I'm sure of it.

I put my hand against the glass once again. Animals like to get your smell, and I want the coyote to get mine for when I come back, for I will. I lean over to the glass and kiss it close to his muzzle, and then I see some little kid standing there looking at me. I guess I get red in the face.

"Coyotes are tame," I tell the little kid and run after my father.

Stephanie wants to know what I liked best, and of course I tell her the coyote. She thinks that is funny, and then she goes into some story about wolves and how Romulus and Remus lived off a wolf and that's how Rome came into being.

We take a long walk through the park and have an ice-cream soda at the fanciest soda place I was ever in, Rumpelmayer's, and Stephanie tells about how she used to come in here all the time when she was a kid. So I guess she is rich. She says that next week I should come to have dinner with them in their apartment, and would I like that. I ask her if I can bring Fred. She says sure. We finish the soda, and she gives me a kiss good-bye as Father and I get into a taxicab for the ride to Mother's.

Fred jumps all over both Father and me when we get home. Mother says she wants Father to stay for a drink with her, but he can't, he says, he and Stephanie have a dinner date in an hour, and he's sorry.

"That's all right, David," Mother says. "Davy and I will be ringing in the New Year. Won't we, darling?" she asks me.

"Sure. And Fred."

Mother and Father think that is very funny.

at one time, and it doesn't make any sense to me that all three have to look alike.

"They'll be at the cleaners all the time if I know boys," Mother says.

"I'm not going to play basketball in them," I tell her.

"Oh, but little boys are always so sweaty," she says, which really makes me mad. I sweat like everyone else, but I'm not a little boy, and people my age don't sweat any more than adults. The man in the school store agrees with every word Mother says though. He even wonders if three blazers will be enough.

"Come on!" I say. "Are you crazy?"

"Davy!" Mother yells. "The gentleman knows whereof he speaks! Apologize."

Can you imagine my mother saying "whereof he speaks"? I get a big laugh from that one and tell the man I know he's not crazy and please pardon me. Mother says I should buy gray flannel pants too and school ties. She is having a ball and tells the man to send the bill to Father.

It is noon by the time I am all checked in at school. I meet two or three teachers at the headmaster's office, and they all tell me they're glad to meet me and hope I will enjoy New York. They're friendly enough. Mother tells all of them that I am "an exceptional boy," and they all tell her that that is nice. If you ask me, she's the exceptional one in the family. She kisses me about ten different times and asks if I like it so far. Sure, I say, since there's nothing not to like yet. I begin to wonder if Mother has enrolled too, since she won't leave and go home. It develops she is waiting to speak to the headmaster, a priest, to tell him she was his sister's college classmate and that they both got an *A* in French conversation. She does that and says she'll see me at home later in the afternoon.

After Mother goes, I get a chance to look around. It's like a public school, I guess, except that everything looks a lot older. There's a lot of dark wood with high varnish on it and a lot of pictures of old priests along the walls in the hallway. It's darker here than any public school I ever saw at home. I meet three or four guys when I go to my first class, which is geography. The teacher says to everyone that the New Year has brought a new pupil and will I stand up to show myself. So I do, and I smile as though I'm friendly, and about everyone smiles back except the kid in the seat in front of me, who doesn't even turn around to see what I look like.

There's no nonsense about getting the class under way though. They have been studying about South America, and Mr. Miller, the teacher, pulls down a lot of maps from a collection of rolled-up ones. There are a whole lot of different things on the maps—one is for elevation, another for population, another for crops and all that stuff.

A big fat kid in the first row of seats raises his hand. "Yes, Malcolm," the teacher says.

"I lived in La Paz, Bolivia."

"You did?" says the teacher.

"Yes."

"Did you like it?"

"I guess so."

"What was it like?"

"I dunno. You know," Malcolm says.

"Would you point out La Paz on the map, Malcolm?" Malcolm edges himself out of his seat and goes to the rainfall map. He looks at it for a while.

"I dunno," he says.

"Look over here at the geographic-boundary map," the teacher says. "That's the more familiar type of map."

Malcolm shuffles to the right map, but he starts giggling after one of the boys laughs at him.

"I dunno," he says again.

Mr. Miller points out the city to Malcolm, who says he knew it was there all the time. He gets a big laugh out of that one and sits down.

"Malcolm was very fortunate to have a chance to live in Bolivia," the teacher says. Then he continues with a lot of stuff about the best way to study a country is to talk with people who have lived there and not rely on books alone. Boy, I'll bet a talk with Malcolm about Bolivia would be edifying. Malcolm is looking around and smiling at everyone until the teacher tells him to pay attention. Malcolm stops smiling, and I can see from the look on his face that he's not happy that the teacher has told him to pay attention. He looks like Fred when I have had to punish him severely, and I feel a little sorry for Malcolm.

The kid in front of me, the one who didn't turn around to see what I looked like, turns around now and says—yes *says*, not whispers—"Quit jerking your leg up and down. I'm about to fall off my seat. Your desk moves my seat."

"I'm sorry," I whisper.

"Don't be sorry. Just stop it," this kid says in a very loud voice.

Mr. Miller interrupts our friendly dialogue. "What's the matter, Altschuler?"

"This new guy is so nervous that he's shaking his desk. I'm going to be on the floor if he doesn't quit it, Mr. Miller," Altschuler says.

Malcolm laughs. He thinks it's a big joke. I guess I get twenty-two shades of red, and I try to mutter that I'm sorry.

"That's all right, Ross," the teacher says to me. "Altschuler can pull his chair closer to his desk if you are agitating it."

"That isn't what's important, Mr. Miller," Altschuler says. "This kid comes in here in the middle of the year and takes Wilkins' seat. Maybe Wilkins will come back. What will you do then?"

I don't know what they're talking about, so I decide that the only thing I can do is say nothing. Mr. Miller says that if Wilkins comes back he can have his old desk back. But since I'm here and the seat behind Altschuler is the only one available in the room, that's where I'm going to sit.

"Just quit bouncing your leg up and down!" Altschuler yells.

I tell him again that I'm sorry, and Altschuler picks up a pencil on his desk and throws it down violently. That is the end of that interruption, and Mr. Miller starts talking about tin mining in the Andes. It's very interesting, the way he presents his story with some slides and a lot of stuff to dramatize how thin the air is up there and how difficult it is to mine there and still keep your health. He makes us close our eyes and imagine we are all in the Andes and have only half as much air available to us as we have in New York.

He says we can get the same feeling those miners have if we hold back every other breath we would breathe normally, and before long I get the idea and so do the other guys, and we all get a little dizzy, in a nice way though. I can see that it would be difficult to be a laborer if you had only half as much air as you can get in New York.

The class after geography is English, and we're supposed to have read Shakespeare's *Julius Caesar* over Christmas. A lady teaches that class, and she says wouldn't it be fun to put on *Julius Caesar*. She says she will do the ladies' parts if we will do all the other parts. She says we don't have to do it according to Shakespeare's text but that we should use the same story line. Everyone thinks that is a good idea. They start talking about what parts they want each other to play. When they select Altschuler to play Brutus, I figure that this teacher may be off on the wrong approach to introducing great plays to kids. Some good-looking kid decides that he is going to be Mark Antony, and no one else speaks up for that part. The funny thing is that no one wants to be Caesar, so they decide I will be Caesar.

"Oh, good, Mr. Ross," Miss Stuart says. "You'll have to read the play tonight. The others are ahead of you."

I tell her that I read the play last year, and she says that is marvelous, and she supposes that in Boston people are far ahead of New Yorkers when it comes to reading Shakespeare.

I tell her I don't know, and I don't. I tell her I have read *The Merchant of Venice* though, and *A Midsummer-Night's Dream* too. She says that that is marvelous, and she hopes I can put up with my backward classmates.

Altschuler decides that he doesn't want to play Brutus. He wants to be Caesar. There's a lot of huff about it, and I say I'll be glad to be Brutus. Miss Stuart says it should be settled by vote, and it ends up that the only people voting for Altschuler to play Caesar are Altschuler and Malcolm. Altschuler looks at me in an unfriendly way, and I wonder if in two hours I have a New York enemy.

The rest of the school day goes by OK, and at three thirty it is time to go home. There are five buses waiting outside the school, marked "East Side—Above 72nd," "East Side—57th-72nd," "East Side—14th-57th," "Greenwich Village," and "West Side—Above 14th." I get on the last bus. I see Altschuler sitting there in the rear seat. He is sitting in the middle so that no one can get to either side of him. I figure that he wants the seat to himself. Maybe he will stretch out and go to sleep, I think. There's no one else on the bus I recognize from my class, so I go to the back of the bus.

"Hi," I say.

Altschuler just looks at me and nods. I sit in one of the seats next to the back one and turn around to Altschuler.

"If you want to be Caesar, it's OK with me," I say.

"You could have voted for me," he answers.

"I didn't vote. I didn't think I should."

"I voted for me," he says. "I would be a much better Caesar than you."

There's one thing about this guy; he's not modest. The second thing is that he says exactly what he's got on his mind. I never met anyone like Altschuler before.

"Well," I say, "it's just that if you want to change parts with me, that's OK."

Altschuler doesn't answer me. He is busy spreading himself all over the back seat. The bus is getting crowded now with a lot of little kids. A couple of them come back to Altschuler's seat, but they take a look at him and go back to select one of the front seats or to stand. The school only goes through the ninth grade, so Altschuler and I are about the oldest people on the bus. I'm the only kid without the school blazer, so I guess this makes me a celebrity. All the little kids look at me about eight times each, and I can hear my name repeated a few times. I try to look as though I don't hear it.

"What's your first name?" I ask Altschuler.

"Everyone calls me Altschuler. Just like everyone will call you Ross," he answers.

"Oh," I say.

Altschuler is quiet for a minute and so am I until he says, "It's Douglas."

"Mine's David," I say. "Everyone calls me Davy though."

"Oh," Altschuler says. "We call each other by our last names here except for Malcolm. Everyone calls him by his first name. He's the only one."

The bus gets started. The kids in the bus going to the East Side between 57th and 72nd yell at us as we pull away. They shout things together as though they are cheering, like "The West Side ain't the best side!" and "You're living your life at the point of a knife." The little kids in my bus yell right back, "If you live East, you're a beast."

I can see right away that I'm going to hear these chants for a long time, so I say to Altschuler, "Is this the only way to get home?"

"It's part of the tuition," he answers. "I walk a lot. I don't live far."

I ask him where he lives and he tells me, and it's the street next to mine, so I say something brilliant like "It's a small world." Altschuler doesn't answer that declaration, and I can't say that I blame him. We get off the bus together at about the fourth stop on the route, and I tell Altschuler that I meant it when I said it was OK with me if he wanted to play Caesar in that dumb play Miss Stuart decided we should put together. He says that he will like playing Brutus. He says that one thing he hates is people who betray friendships and confidences. He will make Brutus appear like a snake in the grass. I tell him that I'd have to read the play again before I could agree that Brutus should be played like a snake in the grass.

"People who betray friends are snakes," Altschuler says. "Good-bye," he says and goes off to his house a block away from mine.

It has begun to get dark by the time I get home, and I am disappointed that it has. I had wanted to take Fred for a long walk today. This is the first day since we got to New York that he has been alone most of the time. When I come in he's crazy to see me and jumps in the air like he's a ballerina, he's so eager to give me a smack and one of his lick jobs. He squirts all over the floor in his excitement. Mother comes to greet me and sees that Fred has beat me to it.

"Cripes!" she declares. "Is there going to be a flood every time you come through the door?"

She turns right around and gets some paper towels from the kitchen. I tell her that I'll take care of it and that it's nothing. I tell her that I'll take Fred out right away so that he won't mess up her floors any more. I tell her that Fred just got excited, that's all. She says sure, sure, sure, and she stumbles a little bit when she bends to wipe up Fred's business. There's not much, just a small puddle no bigger than two or three quarters, but to hear Mother talk about it, Fred has half the Atlantic Ocean in him.

"He did it to me too," she says.

"That's because he was glad to see you."

"That kind of glad I can do without. Go ahead. Take him out."

She gives me a kiss, sort of, and I can tell that she has begun very early to have her before-dinner drinks. Fred and I pounce down the stairs and go for our stroll. When he lifts his leg on the fire hydrant across from the house, I tell him that he is a very good dog for holding so much inside him. He keeps his leg up for three minutes, it seems to me, and it never stops coming. I don't know what Mother got so excited about. He could have left the whole thing up there if he weren't as good a dog as he is.

twelve

Altschuler is waiting for the bus on the corner of my street the next morning. I say hello to him, and he just nods. I ask a lot of dumb questions about whether or not the bus is always on time, and if we will get seats, and what happens if we miss it. Altschuler just shrugs his shoulders or nods his head to answer me, and the less he says the dumber my questions get. I'm angry at him. I'm trying to be friendly, and he's acting like I'm a big annoyance. I'm glad when I see the bus pulling up in five minutes. Altschuler goes right to the rear seat again, and a couple of little kids who were sitting there jump up and move to seats toward the front. I tell myself not to be so friendly and to sit in one of the front seats myself. Altschuler can keep his silence to himself. I don't need it.

"I'm Frankie Menlo," the little kid I sit next to says. "I'm eight."

"I'm Davy Ross."

"I know," Frankie says. "Are you rich?"

"No," I answer.

"Neither am I. I have cousins in New Jersey who are though."

"It's probably fun to visit them."

"I guess so."

"You're probably richer than you think," I say.

"I don't think so. My cousins have a color television set. We don't. Do you?"

"No."

"They also get bigger allowances than I do, even Margaret Mary and she's only five."

"You'll get a bigger allowance someday," I tell Frankie.

"My allowance is adjusted to the United States Government cost-of-living index," he says. "Last week it was a dollar and eighteen cents. My father wants me to be a businessman."

I ask him if they call him Menlo at school or Frankie. He says they won't call him Menlo until the fifth grade, but I can call him Menlo. He's a pretty bright little kid, and I tell him I'd be glad to call him Menlo if he wants me to. He asks if I will sit with him every morning. I look around at Altschuler, who has himself spread out in the back of the bus as though he owns it, and I tell Menlo that I'll sit with him a lot but maybe not every morning. He says that will be fine, and then he tells me that he likes me a lot. The bus has arrived at school.

"I like you too, Menlo," I tell him, which I am glad to

do since he's the first person to exert himself and welcome me to this school. I don't care if he's only eight.

Menlo takes hold of my hand when we get out of the bus, and we walk toward the school together. Menlo runs ahead to tell some other little kids his own age about me. I know he does because he keeps pointing to me as they stand around outside. I pass them, and he says, "See you on the bus this afternoon, Ross."

"Right, Menlo," I say.

The kid smiles, and all his friends look at him and me with a sort of envious look. I can hear them calling him Frankie, and I guess that Frankie has taken several leaps ahead in his buddies' eyes now that an old kid like me calls him Menlo.

I don't feel so conspicuous in school on the second day, and a couple of the guys ask me to sit next to them during morning chapel, which is only for about fifteen minutes and isn't bad. The priest reads a couple of things from the Bible, and we say a few prayers and sing two hymns. I know the Lord's Prayer of course, so I can say that one OK, but I don't know the other prayers. I guess that I'll have to learn a whole lot of prayers before long. Davy the monk. And I don't know the hymns either. Even if I did, I wouldn't sing them, being the hummer that I am from way back. It's worse now because my voice cracks all the time. Boy, me and puberty!

I see Altschuler waiting outside when we leave chapel and I ask him if everyone doesn't have to go. He says it's optional for non-Episcopalians.

"It is?" I say. "I didn't know that. I thought everyone had to go."

"No."

"What are you?" I ask.

For a few seconds he looks at me as though I'm crazy. I wonder if I've asked something no one ever asked him before. Kids at home used to know what everyone was because there were only so many things you could be in a little town. Or you could be nothing, of course, except for Christmas and Easter, and then you could choose from a lot of churches, as I frequently did. My grandmother did too, though she went to church more than twice a year. Come to think of it, she would go to one church several times in a row, then go to another one in the same way. She got involved with the Methodists, the Unitarians, the Catholics, and the Congregationalists, and she got a lot of mail from all of them, asking her to contribute to building funds. Churches in my town were always building new schools or community halls or new churches even.

After Altschuler has had his fill of staring at me, he says, "I'm an agnostic."

"What's that?"

"It's someone who doesn't know if there's a God or not."

"Do you have special churches?"

"Agnostics don't go to church. The point of being an agnostic is that you're not certain if there should be any churches."

"Oh," I say. "Are your parents agnostics too?"

Altschuler looks at me again as though he doesn't believe the question I asked, but finally he says, "We don't talk about religion at home. It's a personal thing for us to make up our own minds about."

I tell Altschuler that I guess I'm an agnostic too, but that I've never thought very much about it. I tell him about my church-going habits, which are not regular, as I explained, and that people in my family seemed to move from one church to the other without bringing God's wrath down on them. By this time we are in the algebra class, and Altschuler is talking to me in a regular if not friendly way, so I sit behind him after I introduce myself to the teacher.

The rest of the day goes by fine, though Altschuler doesn't have anything else to say to me. When it's time for physical education, we go to this crummy dark gymnasium in the school's basement and change into shorts and T-shirts for basketball. Altschuler is the class jock, it develops, and he plays circles around everyone. I just sort of mess around, and no one goes batty when I manage to sink a few long ones. Malcolm is the class clown on the basketball floor as well as in the classroom. He can't dribble. He bounces the ball on the floor once but can't bring his hand and the ball together again, so he makes a big joke of it and tells me that he hates basketball. He says he's a good football player and I should see him playing guard on the varsity team next fall. Malcolm is two times the size of any of the other kids, so I suppose the school sits him down in the middle of the line and figures opposing teams will have a rough time just getting around him. Malcolm laughs a lot whenever he gets the basketball by accident. All the kids yell at him when that happens. "Toss it here, Malcolm!" "Let's have the ball, Malcolm!" Everyone knows that Malcolm will never try to lob in a basket.

Miss Stuart is all ready to go into rehearsal with our production of *Julius Caesar* and says the first thing we have to do is write the script. Everyone who is playing a part has to write his own part, and in that way we'll be sure to get the most out of the play. Some of the guys are playing murderers and that's all, so they're going to have a pretty easy week. People like me and Altschuler and the good-looking kid who's going to be Mark Antony have to do a lot of work though, and I'm sorry that I got elected.

We start to talk about the play and about the character of the various people who took part in the events surrounding Caesar's murder and about how Shakespeare thought of them, and before you know it everyone is very down on Caesar. Altschuler is telling them how Caesar wants to rule forever, and I pipe in with the fact that Caesar deserved the gratitude of the Roman people for leading them in so many battles and getting so much of the world for them and all that. Altschuler says that Caesar was like Hitler, which really turns all the guys against me, and we haven't decided anything before the class is over. Miss Stuart says that we'll begin to write the script tomorrow.

At three thirty when I go out to the bus, Altschuler is standing there, waiting outside the bus door. I say hello to him.

"Do you want to walk home?" he asks.

I am surprised and don't say anything. Then I hear a tapping on the window next to the first seat. It's the kid Frankie Menlo. I wave to him, and he waves back, a big smile on his face.

"I don't know. I have to get home to walk my dog," I say to Altschuler.

"OK," he says and then turns away from me a little bit. Frankie Menlo has stuck his face against the window and is waiting for me. I go up the first step of the bus.

"Hi, Menlo," I say to him.

"Hi, Ross," he answers. "I saved a seat for you."

I go up into the aisle. A lot of little kids are looking from Frankie to me, wondering if I'll sit down. Frankie pats the seat as though he is going to make it more comfortable for me to sit on. I look back out the door and see that Altschuler has moved away a few feet and is beginning to walk away.

"Menlo," I say, "thanks for the seat. I'm going to walk."

Frankie looks as though I dumped boiling water on his face, so I say, "Save me a seat in the morning, Menlo. OK?"

He doesn't answer, and I run off the bus in a second. I call to Altschuler and ask him to wait up. He keeps walking but slows down a little and I catch up to him.

"I thought you had to walk your dog," he says.

"I do."

"It doesn't take so long to walk home anyway. On some days I'm there almost as fast as the bus."

We walk along for a few minutes in silence. The bus

with Frankie Menlo on it pulls by, and I raise my hand to wave to Frankie. But he's looking the other way. I wonder if it's on purpose. Not that it matters. But I am sorry to disappoint the kid.

"There's this little kid on the bus," I start telling Altschuler. "He's really a bright little kid. We had a talk together this morning, and he wanted me to ride home with him."

"Yes," Altschuler says. "I saw him."

I tell him about Frankie's allowance and the cost-of-living thing connected with it. I tell him I think that's pretty funny, to have an eight-year-old kid on an allowance with a cost-of-living clause. I ask Altschuler if he doesn't think that's funny, and he shrugs his shoulders. I begin to be sorry that I didn't ride with Menlo. At least with him there's some conversation, to say nothing of the fact that Frankie looks at me as though I am a big deal.

So I start looking around the street where we are walking. Altschuler knows the direction all right, so I just tag along with him.

It's warm out, and the sun is shining. It's January thaw, and now that I'm walking, I'm in no rush. The street we are on is crowded. A lot of the people are only a few years older than me, and they look friendly. I ask Altschuler why some of them look so dirty, and he tells me they are hippies. I have read about hippies a lot of course, as who hasn't, but I've never seen any. A couple of the dirty-looking guys are wearing American Indian clothes and beads, and I ask Altschuler if they are Indians. He laughs, and I think that is the first time he has laughed at something I said, so I laugh too. He tells me that the real hippies are on the East Side, not here on Eighth Street. Someday if we have time, he will take me to see them. He laughs again when he says maybe we can let our hair grow for *Julius Caesar* and put on a hippie production of the play for Miss Stuart.

It happens that while Altschuler is turning into this big comedian I am occupying myself with staring at someone, trying to decide if it's a boy or a girl. I'm not even polite about it, and I can almost hear my grandmother telling me that no one on earth should be looked at as a curiosity but only out of curiosity or friendship. Now I know what she meant because I'm looking at this person in a way Grandmother wouldn't have liked. And the person knows it.

"It's love, baby," the person says. "That's what it's all about. You gotta wear flowers in your hair."

And then the person laughs gently as I hurry on because I don't have anything to say and am too much of a coward to apologize for staring.

"Did you see?" I ask Altschuler.

He nods that he did.

"I'm sorry I stared. I've never seen anyone like that before."

"You have to keep your cool," Altschuler says.

"What's that?"

"You shouldn't get excited just because people don't look like other people."

"I'm not excited or anything like that," I say. "Did you know if it was a boy or a girl?"

"I didn't notice."

"Didn't notice! How could you not notice? I mean the person had all this hair, and the way the person was shaped you couldn't tell, the sweater was so baggy. Is there a lot of that?"

Altschuler tells me that he guesses there is a lot of everything in New York and that I shouldn't be so sur-prised at the things I see on the street. He tells me that he doesn't even notice things he was afraid of when he was a kid. He tells me that he used to get frightened when he saw a person lying asleep on the sidewalk but that he is not scared of that anymore.

"Asleep on the sidewalk!" I say.

"Sure. A lot of times you see people lying on the sidewalk or in a doorway. That's because they are drunks."

He goes on to tell me about all the places these sleepers can go to live for a night or two if they want to. Places like the Salvation Army. He tells me that a lot of them like to go to jail, but it's hard to get in these days just for drinking. You have to toss a brick through a window or something like that. Then they will take you into jail for a few weeks and give you food and a bed. He says that's why so many store windows get broken in cold weather. Windows aren't broken in the summer because the jails don't have air-conditioning. That's why so many drinking people are on the sidewalk in hot weather, he says.

"Maybe they aren't all drinking people," I say. "Maybe some of them are sick."

"That's what I thought at first."

"Couldn't it be that way?"

"No," Altschuler says.

We are walking up Sixth Avenue now, and we pass this candy shop with a lot of glass jars filled with wrapped candies in the window. I stop to look at the jars because I like candy. Altschuler tells me to come on if I want to walk with him.

"Dougie!" a lady says from inside the store. "Dougie! I haven't seen you since before Thanksgiving!"

This lady rushes out from the store and grabs hold of Altschuler. Altschuler stands there looking awkward and embarrassed. The lady gives him sort of a kiss, and Altschuler looks even more embarrassed.

"Oh, Dougie," she says, "I've missed you so. And Larry, poor boy. How is he?"

"He's home again."

"That's good news?" the lady asks.

"I don't know."

The lady starts to sigh, and then I think she is crying. She says it isn't fair that anything should happen to such a nice boy. There are plenty of hoodlums on the street, she says, that something terrible like that should happen to. She says there's no reasoning with God's will.

Altschuler is just nodding at the lady. He doesn't have anything to say to her, and he looks at me as though he blames me for stopping in front of the candy store. The lady sees me then too.

"So? Who's this? Another Larry?"

Altschuler moves away from the store.

"How do you do," the lady says. "I'm Dougie's friend. And Larry's. If you're their friend, you're mine too."

She holds out her hand and shakes mine. I tell her that I am new in New York and that Altschuler and I are in the same class and we live in the same neighborhood. I tell her that I don't know Larry.

"So? Already he's forgotten," she says.

"I just moved here. I never knew him," I tell her.

"That Larry," the lady says, "oh, he's quite a boy. Dougie and Larry came in every Friday for seven years, didn't you, Dougie?"

Altschuler nods. He is walking away, so I tell the lady that I am glad to meet her, and she says that I should come into the store the next time and that I should bring Dougie with me. She doesn't like to conduct her social life on the sidewalk, she says.

"Poor Larry," she says as we walk on, and she goes back into her store. I can hear her take a deep breath and sigh. Altschuler doesn't say anything, and I don't figure that I should ask any questions. We walk without speaking for about ten minutes, and then we are at my corner. I stop and tell Altschuler that this is where I will leave him.

"Larry lives in my apartment house," Altschuler says suddenly. "You are sitting in his seat in most of our classes. He had to stop coming to class just before Christmas. We always went to school together, ever since we were about three. Something happened to his blood. He gets tired all the time. He's supposed to die this month."

I don't know what to say. Altschuler is standing there,

expecting me to say he won't die or something like that, but I don't have anything at all to say. I want to say I'm sorry, but I know from when Grandmother died that that is a dumb thing to say about dying, so I just stand there like a twirp and look at Altschuler, who looks at me for a minute and then walks off toward his block.

thirteen

Before I know it, it's Saturday and I'm supposed to go over to my father and Stephanie's to have dinner with them. Fred is delighted that when I leave the apartment with my father he is invited too. My father has come in the middle of the afternoon. It has been arranged between my mother and him that she will be out shopping, and I'm glad of that. Mother has been saying regularly, like every night since New Year's Eve, that she prefers to deal with Father at a distance and that that is the only civilized way to act in situations like hers. I don't know what she's talking about most of the time, because I know that she would like my father to have stayed with her for one of her damned drinks when he brought me home a week ago.

Father lives near Central Park, so Fred has his first genuine New York treat. From the way he begins to whimper in the taxicab when we get within a few blocks of the park,

I have the eerie feeling that he knows where we are going. It's not as warm as it was last week, but there are still a lot of people in the park. It is quiet there, almost like the country. The roads are blocked off to automobiles on weekends, so Father and I decide that it is OK to let Fred off his leash. He bolts away as though he had been kept in a cage for years. For half a minute I get worried that he will run off and get lost, except I can see that Fred keeps looking to see me and zooms back to run a wide circle around me if he gets too far away from us. Fred goes batty; he is having such a good time. He keeps throwing himself on the ground to roll over in one delectable smell after another. I can guess what he is going to smell like after the sixth or seventh roll. He is having such a good time though that I don't want to stop him.

A little kid runs over to pet him, and he jumps up and licks the ice-cream mess left around her lips. She thinks that is the funniest thing she ever saw and falls onto the ground so that Fred can get better licks. The kid's mother doesn't think it's funny though.

"Pooky!" the lady yells. "Dirty girl! What are you doing with that dirty dog?"

She grabs the kid from the ground and whacks her rear end. Fred is mystified. The kid begins to cry and babble away about the doggie at the same time. She is looking back at Fred and holding her arm out toward him as her mother drags her away. Fred runs right along with them until the lady yells at him to go away. Fred is surprised and growls a little. When I hear this, I run right over to him.

"The dog should be on a leash!" the lady shrieks. "It's against the law to have him off the leash. There's no telling what he might have done to Pooky!"

"I'm sorry," I mutter as I bend down to Fred to hold him back from his new friend, who wants him even more now that her mother has told me she's going to send me to jail if I don't watch out. I pick up Fred and carry him over to my father. In half a minute the lady and the kid have disappeared down a path in the opposite direction, so I put Fred down and my father and I have a good laugh. Fred jumps all over us, which is, I guess, his way of laughing.

We mess around in the park for a long time. My father is all the time picking up sticks, pieces of branches from trees, and throwing them twenty or thirty feet in front of him. Fred wants to chase after them, but he won't do it until I say "Go get it, Fred. Bring it here." I hope my father doesn't mind if Fred won't run after the stick unless I tell him to. And when he brings it back, it's to me, not Father.

A lot of dogs are off leash in the park, and Fred enjoys running up to big ones in particular and barking at them as though he is going to take them apart. A great dane starts to get frisky with Fred, who proves to be a real coward and zooms back for the protection he thinks I give him. The great dane follows Fred and jumps all over me and licks me like Fred, except that his tongue is about six times the size of Fred's and he's so strong that I'm almost on the ground before his master calls him back. When he is a safe distance away, Fred starts barking and growling at him again. I tell Fred he's all noise and no action. He doesn't understand

and walks along next to us like a real hero protecting the defenseless.

We are near the zoo now. I see that among the many things prohibited in the zoo are dogs.

"They would excite the animals," Father says.

"Fred?" I ask.

"You know how he can bark."

"What if I put his leash back on?" I do that in spite of my father's dubious look, and we march into the zoo. No one stops us or looks at us strangely, so we decide that it's OK as long as Fred doesn't start acting crazy. We walk past a couple of zebras in their cages and a lot of deer. Fred loves the smell, and I think he would be delighted if we would let him spend the rest of the day there. Some kids are holding out their hands to feed junk to the deer, even though there are signs everywhere telling you not to feed the animals. I conclude that a lot of sign painters paint a lot of signs no one pays any attention to. Including me.

I drag Fred away from the deer, past a camel. I don't think Fred sees the camel, he is so tall, because Fred doesn't even nod in that direction. We turn the corner, and there is a row of wolves and wild dogs and things like that. Fred's hackles bristle right away, so I decide that we shouldn't walk down that row. We go instead to a big pool in the middle of the zoo to look at the seals. There are four of them. Two of them are sunning themselves on a concrete island in the middle of the pool, and two of them are swimming around in the water. People are standing there laughing at the seals for no particular reason. In a minute, after my father and I have stood watching them, we start to laugh too. I don't ask myself why, except that the seals on the island remind me of Fred. They are staring in my direction, looking me squarely in the eye.

"You want to see your cousins, Fred?" I say. Fred is so low down that he can't see over the edge of the pool, and he's whining away to get a look at what everyone else is looking at. I pick up Fred at just the moment one of the seals lets out a high creepy honking sound which delights Fred. He lets out a sound almost like it. I've only heard Fred bark and whine before. I've never heard him honk. I'm surprised for a second.

"Was that you?" I ask Fred, who's squirming in my arms.

The seal honks again, and so does Fred. By now, all the people on our side of the pool are looking at Fred and laughing at him more than at the seals. Fred is trying to wiggle out of my arms and into the pool to have a long honk with his friend on that island, I guess, so I put him down on the ground. He immediately jumps up to the rim of the pool, which must be three times his height. I'm so surprised that I almost lose hold of his leash. Father just manages to grab Fred before he jumps into the pool.

The seal and Fred continue to honk away at each other, and it is no small effort to drag Fred out of the zoo. He keeps tugging at his leash to get back to the pool, and it is almost ten minutes before we can get him to calm down and behave himself.

"Honk for Stephanie," I keep urging Fred when we get to my father's apartment. "Show Stephanie how you honk."

Fred doesn't know what I am talking about, and when I try to make a honking noise myself to demonstrate what I want him to do, he tilts his head to indicate that he thinks I am crazy. Stephanie thinks Fred is funny and that what happened in the zoo was funny and that the way Fred licks her is particularly funny, so she has a good time rolling all over the floor with Fred. I guess Fred thinks she's the Queen of Sheba, because he won't pay any attention to me and my father as soon as he has rolled around with Stephanie awhile. Of course, it helps that she keeps going into the kitchen every so often to look at some meat she is roasting. Maybe Fred thinks she's making his supper.

In a way she is. When it comes time for dinner, Fred sits himself right next to Stephanie's chair. He has been taught never to beg food from the table, so he doesn't forget himself to the extent of doing anything as terrible as that. He just keeps his eyes fastened on Stephanie, who wants to know how I resist feeding him when he looks as though there is nothing in the world that would make him happier than a piece of roast beef.

"Sure," I tell her. "It would make him happy all right. But you'd have to keep on making him happy. If he gets you to give him some stuff, you'll never eat another mouthful without having him look at you like you were robbing it from him. Isn't that right, Fred? Don't I know you?"

Fred knows I'm talking about him, so he ignores me. He just keeps on looking at Stephanie. He has sized her up right. When she is about half-finished with her roast beef, I can see her cutting up the rest of it into small bite-size morsels. Fred hears her too. He stands up and practically pushes Stephanie out of her seat. She takes her plate to the kitchen. If she had broken her stride into the kitchen, Fred would have bashed into her in half a second, he is so close to her. In a minute I can hear his jaws smacking together as Stephanie gives him the best part of her dinner.

"It sounds like real love," I say to my father.

"They make a noisy couple," my father says.

"Just at dinner time."

"I guess they'd be noisy if they started barking at each other too."

"Stephanie doesn't bark," I say.

"You don't think so?" my father says. "You should come around more often if you believe that."

"OK. I will."

"You can come around as often as you wish, Davy," my father says. "We want to have you with us whenever you want to be."

Stephanie comes back into the room, followed closely by her new admirer. She says, "I wish I had had two homes in New York when I was thirteen. That's the way to look at it, Davy."

"OK," I say. And then no one says anything. "It's OK with Fred too."

The three of us sort of laugh. Fred has taken himself to a new position, next to my father's chair. I have the feeling that in a minute I'm going to hear my father cutting up the rest of his meat.

fourteen

"What did Stephanie have with her roast beef, Davy?" Mother asks and asks again after I tell her that she had a lot of stuff.

"What kind of stuff?"

"You know," I tell her, "vegetables and bread and that stuff."

"What vegetables?"

"I don't know. Vegetables!"

"Did she have potatoes?"

"I don't think so," I say. "No, she didn't. She had beans, I think."

"Beans! What kind? Yellow? Green?"

"Green."

"How were they prepared?"

And I tell my mother that I don't know how they were prepared. They were just beans. Beans are beans. What does she think I did, go out in my father's kitchen and watch Stephanie make the supper? And Mother says that all she wanted to know was if they were fresh beans or were they frozen. I tell her how do I know? She gets mad and says it's all right not to tell her anything if that's the way I want it. What did I come to New York for if it wasn't to have a good time with her and to share everything together?

"I'm sorry, Mother. I don't know about all that stuff in the kitchen. Ask Fred. He spent most of his time out there with her."

I think that's kind of funny, so I bend down to Fred and ask him to tell Mother what kind of beans Stephanie had with the roast beef tonight and how were they prepared? And did he see her take them out of a frozen package or did they come out of the big bean garden they have growing in the back part of my father's apartment?

Mother doesn't think I'm such a funny fellow though. "That's all right, young man," she says. "It probably doesn't mean anything to you that I was home here alone all afternoon and that I had dinner by myself, knowing that it was important for me to give up my evening so that I would be here when you came home. The least I could have expected from you was for you to share with me what appears to have been a very pleasant day."

"Come on, Mother," I say.

"Don't 'come on' me, Davy! You're just lucky you have a home to come home to and a loving mother waiting for you! You're just lucky..."

She starts to go on, but I guess I look at her with surprise mapped out all over my face.

"Oh, dear, Davy," she goes on, "I didn't mean it like it sounded. Of course you have a home. Of course I'll wait here for you. You know that, don't you, dear?"

"Sure," I say. We look at each other without saying anything for a long time. The trouble with a New York apartment is that there isn't anyplace you can turn to to wait for something like what was happening between Mother and me to pass. Mother turns away and then back. She says she'll get a cold drink for me if I want one. Do I want one? she asks me two times, and I say No. The third time I say Yes, and she tells me she knew I did. She wants to get it for me. She wants one too.

She messes around out there in the kitchen. I can hear two or three ice cubes hit the floor, followed by Mother's kitchen oaths. Oath time usually comes with the cocktail hour for Mother, and I guess from the way she smells and from her lively curiosity about Stephanie's dinner, Mother has been sitting around having a lot of cold drinks.

"Dear Davy," Mother starts when she gets back in the room, "I'm sorry I sounded so harsh a minute ago. You know that I get carried away at times, don't you, dear?"

I tell her that sure I do, and I'm sorry that I didn't answer her questions about dinner when she asked them, and that in addition to beans Stephanie had a green salad, rolls from Pepperidge Farm, and carrots with some goo on them. I tell her that they drank a bottle of wine and I had

Diet Pepsi because I didn't feel like having milk. We had fancy peaches for dessert.

Mother just says, "Oh," and that's all. The great desire to hear about the meal has dissipated itself, and we both take big swallows of our cold drinks.

"She's big around the middle, don't you think?" Mother says.

"Who?"

"Stephanie, of course. She's always seemed rather bovine to me, don't you agree?"

I ask her what she means by bovine, and she says she means that Stephanie looks like a big cow. Would I agree? I don't say anything. I think about Stephanie for a minute and remember that she rolled all over the floor with Fred. I don't think Mother would do that. I don't think.

"Would you roll over the floor with Fred?" I ask Mother.

"What?"

"Would you get down there with him and roll around?"

"I would not," Mother says. "Isn't it enough that he lives here?" She makes a big dent in her drink once again and goes back to the kitchen to fix it. "What a silly damned question," Mother calls back from the kitchen. "What on earth would I want to roll around the floor with Fred for?"

"Oh, I don't know. I wondered if you would."

"Davy!" Mother yells from the kitchen. "She didn't!" Mother runs back with a new drink. "Did Stephanie roll around with Fred?"

I sort of shrug my shoulders, as noncommittal as I can be.

"She did!" Mother goes on. "The big toadie! She rolled around with Fred just to make you think she liked him. And you fell for it!"

Mother thinks that she's saying the funniest things in the world, and she laughs like a TV comedian laughing at his own jokes. I don't say anything, because if I said what I wanted to say, Mother would toss her drink in my face. No, she wouldn't do that. It's too precious. But she might bop me over the head with today's paper. I sit on the floor next to Fred.

"It isn't such a big deal, getting down here with Fred," I say. "All you have to do is sit on the floor. He must get kind of sick of looking up all the time, don't you think? He probably gets a crick in the neck from looking up at people. Right, Fred? Is that the way it is?" Fred jumps up and licks my face. He moves himself around so that he plops himself solidly in place in my lap. He is the perfect adapter. His body is so long and flexible that whenever I move a muscle he is able to move one too. I lie back on the floor.

"Get up, Davy," Mother says. "It's dirty on the floor."

I don't say anything.

"Davy," she says with emphasis, "I think you should get up."

Fred has crawled up over my body and arranged himself all along my chest and below my waist, stretched out like one of those animal statues guarding an Egyptian tomb. He lowers his head so that his nose is up against my chin, and he pretends to be asleep, sure he has found a bed for the night. I close my eyes too.

"Davy," Mother says, "I want you to get up! You understand that, don't you?"

I don't say anything. I put my arms around Fred, and he makes a purring sound. I remember that I have told him before that I think he's part cat, so I smile. I can hear Mother rush into the kitchen to get herself another drink. When she comes back, she isn't as shook up as when she left. I have opened my eyes, and we are looking at each other. It is straight now between us. I have never looked at anyone like I look at Mother, and I wonder if she has looked at anyone in this way before either.

"Do you want me to love your Fred?" Mother asks. "Is that all there is to it?"

"Not if you don't."

"I don't, Davy. He's part of you. So I want him in my home."

"You could learn to love him."

"Some people aren't animal people."

"You could learn."

"It's unnatural, sweetheart. You don't love unless you can be loved back."

I hold Fred tighter, as though to ask don't you think this doggie loves me?

"Don't measure me against Stephanie because I don't roll around with Fred," Mother says.

"Come down to Fred," I urge my mother. We are still

looking at each other as though we have never seen one another before.

"No, baby," she says. She plays around with her cold drink, rattling the ice in it, and then drinks half of it.

fifteen

It had taken us longer than a week to write the script for Miss Stuart's production of *Julius Caesar*, and in the middle of the second week we had been working on it we had still not managed to come to the point in the play when all the senators murder Caesar. So Miss Stuart said it was time we stopped talking about our respective characters and did something about the play to move it along faster. Altschuler spent so much time convincing everyone that Caesar was an old bastard that the good-looking kid playing Mark Antony, who was dumb, couldn't think up any reasons for honoring Caesar's memory. The play would end with my death, everyone agreed. Everyone but Miss Stuart. She said we had to follow Shakespeare's plot because that was the whole reason for putting on the play this way in the first place. Altschuler said that the only fair thing was to vote, so the class voted in favor of the play ending when

Caesar is killed. The only ones voting against that ending were me and Malcolm, whose sympathies always seemed to be with the underdog. Even Mark Antony voted for the new ending, so Miss Stuart said OK, and we put on the play for the whole school on the second Friday I was there. I was pretty good. The little kids booed me a lot, so I know that I played Caesar just as Altschuler wanted. Altschuler got a big hand at the end. Miss Stuart said it was a waste of her time because Brutus isn't supposed to be the hero. Altschuler told her life is filled with surprises.

That afternoon when everyone is piling into the bus to go home, my young buddy, Frankie Menlo, is waiting for me next to the door. He asks me how come Caesar got killed in the play and that was the end of it. He says that on television the play didn't end that way. Brutus is the villain on television, not Caesar. I tell Menlo about the vote and about how much longer we spent putting the play together than Miss Stuart wanted us to and about how Caesar probably wasn't such a kind gentleman anyway.

Altschuler comes along and says he is going to walk home today if I want to come with him. He tells Menlo he can come too. Menlo beams and suddenly thinks Brutus is the greatest hero who ever walked the earth.

"You mean it? I can walk home with you?" the kid says.

"Sure," Altschuler says.

Menlo runs onto the bus. I can hear him yelling to all his buddies that he's walking with Altschuler and Ross today, so the bus shouldn't wait up for him. The driver asks him what he thinks he's talking about. He tells Menlo that

Altschuler and I live about half a mile from school, while he, Menlo, lives about four miles away, somewhere up on Riverside Drive.

"That's all right," Menlo swears. "I don't mind walking the rest of the way by myself."

"You won't get home until tomorrow morning," the driver tells him.

"No, no," Menlo yells. "Ross and Altschuler said I could walk with them."

"You may never get home!" the driver threatens. "Do you know what happens to rich kids walking the streets alone in the middle of New York?"

Menlo doesn't ask for the answer but only looks at the driver and walks to the door.

"I'll give you guys a rain check on that walk," he says. "I have to be home early today."

The driver thinks Menlo is funny and laughs very loud. Menlo looks at him as though he wants to wrap the steering wheel around his neck and then waves back at Altschuler and me.

"See you, Altschuler," he yells as though we are a hundred yards away. "See you, Ross."

Altschuler and I walk along without saying anything. When we come to the avenue where Altschuler's friend has the candy shop, he crosses over to the other side of the street so we won't pass in front of the shop.

"Everyone liked the play," I say. "Or everyone who spoke to me about it."

"I'm sorry you had to come out on the short end," Altschuler says.

"Oh, that's OK. I guess Miss Stuart won't let us do that again anyway. She was pretty mad about it ending when Caesar is killed."

Altschuler laughs. "That's history for you."

I laugh too. And then we don't say anything for another few minutes.

"Did I tell you that Larry Wilkins died yesterday?" Altschuler says.

"No," I answer.

"He did."

"Oh," I say.

"I'll be going to his funeral tomorrow. That's when it's going to be. I saw him the day before. He was just asleep all the time."

"Oh."

We don't say anything else now but just walk along fast toward home. I don't know what I'm supposed to tell Altschuler, because I don't want to slobber all over him on account of Wilkins, whom I never knew. It would be like me trying to tell him about Grandmother and expecting that he would understand the way I thought of her, like her getting Fred for me, for example, and all the other things she did, and I did, which made it possible for Grandmother and me to be friends. Some things are personal. When you talk about them, they lose the private quality which makes them important.

"Maybe you'd like to meet my dog Fred," I say when we get to my corner. "He's great."

"Sure," Altschuler says.

Altschuler follows me down my street. I ring my door-bell five or six times in short and long beeps and in a variety of sounds and combinations so that old Fred can get excited about me coming home from school. Mother isn't usually home when I come in, on account of her job. She works uptown somewhere, in advertising. But she's home a lot too, working there, writing stuff for her job. She's all the time griping that her job saps her of her creative energies and doesn't leave her enough time to write the important things she knows she is capable of. I'm muttering something about this to Altschuler, trying to explain why it's OK for me to play this symphony I'm playing on the door-bell for Fred while I'm digging into my pocket and hunting for my keys. I get the keys and open the front door, but not before giving another long beep on the doorbell for Fred. By this time the crazy old dog is barking away like a gorilla, and when the front door is opened, I can hear him jumping up against the door inside the apartment, waiting for me to come and claim him.

"Don't be afraid if he barks at you for a minute or two," I tell Altschuler. "He is suspicious of everyone he doesn't know."

I open the door, and Fred runs out into the hallway and jumps all over me and squirts a little on the floor. He sees Altschuler standing behind me and doesn't bark at all. He jumps on him, just as he did on me, and lets another little squirt pop out onto the floor. Altschuler bends down to Fred and rubs him under the muzzle for a second until Fred runs back to me. We go into the apartment with Fred jumping all over both of us, one at a time.

"My mother isn't home. If she were, you would have heard her tell me something about the bestiality of dogs by now."

We both get a laugh from that one, and I explain to Altschuler about how often Fred got to go out in Massachusetts, and how he sometimes gets out only three times a day here in New York and then for only ten or fifteen minutes, and how difficult it has been for Fred to learn to contain himself over such a long period of time, so if he doesn't mind, we will take Fred out right away so that he can do his business. Altschuler says fine, so the three of us trot back downstairs. I put Fred's leash on him, and we take the doggie out for his late afternoon. Fred lifts his leg about four times in the first minute out, and I know how hard it has been for him to hold back, so I tell him how good he has been, and before I know it, Altschuler is telling him the same thing, and we both have another big laugh.

"How would you feel if you could make only three times a day?" I ask.

"I don't know," Altschuler says.

"So what are we laughing about? This is a serious matter." We laugh.

Fred, emptied, now has time to look at Altschuler, and I can see right away that Fred approves of him. He works himself around so that he will walk between us, except when he wants to sniff out something some other dog has left behind. Altschuler says isn't that unsanitary, and I tell him that maybe it is, but it's very dog.

"Right, Fred?" I ask.

Fred jumps into the gutter—surprise!—and plops. For three weeks he has been plopping in a variety of places, a couple of times right in the middle of the sidewalk. On those occasions I have been very angry with him, and he knew it. In my mind, I had compromised on the small dirt plots around the trees planted on the block, because it seemed dangerous to me to walk him in the streets themselves. Some drivers speed even in city streets, and some of them pass slow cars without bothering to see if there are dangers. I had just about given up on having Fred plop in the street, which is where he should and *good* dogs do. One of the things Fred does when he is plopping is to look at me with his is-this-OK-boss? look, and because I love him so much I don't really care what he does so long as no one is hurt or significantly bothered. I always say goofy things like "That's my wonderful doggie" or "Oh, look at what a good dog Fred is," and he finishes and we both go on feeling we have done the right thing by each other. But on this occasion, when Fred has plopped in the gutter, something special is called for. So I bend over and rub him and tell him what an amazing creature he is and so forth. Altschuler looks away like I'm crazy, so of course I have to give him the background. And then he bends over and tells Fred he is wonderful. Fred jumps up and gives Altschuler two licks on the face.

Fred gets to have a longer walk than usual, and when Altschuler and I bring him back to the house it is getting dark. My mother has come home, and she begins to tell me from the other room how worried she was about me and Fred. She finally stops talking long enough so that I can call to her that I have a guest.

"Who is it?" she calls.

"It's Douglas Altschuler," I call back. "From school."

"Hello, Douglas," she says.

Altschuler just stands there.

"Douglas, hello," she says.

"Hello, Mrs. Ross," he calls out.

"The *first* Mrs. Ross," she yells, then laughs. She comes into the living room from the kitchen. Her hand is held out to Altschuler, and they shake hands. They tell each other how glad they are to meet each other, but Fred wants none of this. He has a few special toys he likes to have me try to get away from him, his hard ball and an old rag of a T-shirt I have knotted up for him which he grabs between his teeth as though I want to get it from him. He likes me to chase him around the apartment, trying to get these things away from him. Sometimes he works it so that I will get them and then toss them into another room where he can run after them and play the whole keep-away-from-Davy game all over again. Fred has grabbed the T-shirt this time and flaunts it before me and Altschuler, wanting one of us to grab it, or try to grab it, from him.

"I'm so glad Davy has a school chum in the neighborhood," Mother says. "You can be friends, can't you?"

Altschuler and I both mutter something indistinct to Mother and to ourselves.

"Of course you'll be friends!" Mother declares, ever the gentle urger. "Ask him to come over to play with you tomorrow, Davy."

I know that this is a game. Mother knows that Father has been getting me on Saturdays for the last few weeks, so if Altschuler is here it will make it awkward for everyone.

"I can't, Mrs. Ross," Altschuler says. "I'm doing something else tomorrow." And I remember about Wilkins, whose seat I occupy in most of my classes.

"Well, you'll be good friends, won't you?" Mother says.

Altschuler tells me that he thinks Fred is great and it would be fun to get to know him better. His mother won't let him have a dog because of it being the city and all, and he'd really like to have one someday. Mother says that Altschuler should listen to his mother about everything and that Mrs. Altschuler is obviously a lot smarter than Mrs. Ross. Mother thinks that she has cracked a big joke, and she carries it further when she tells Fred not to worry, that she wouldn't think of breaking up the love affair of the century.

Altschuler says that he has to go home now, that he is late. Mother says he must stay for dinner and the three of us will have a card game after.

"We'll do anything you want, Douglas," Mother says.

Altschuler says that that would be nice some other time, but not tonight. Mother says OK, he can suit himself, but that he has a home away from home any time he wants it.

Mother the gracious hostess is someone I don't know so well, so it takes me quite a bit of time to collect my thoughts after Altschuler has gone. A home away from home, she told him, and he hadn't even been here for a half hour. And what about me? I have only talked with the guy a few times plus the two walks home from school. Plus I admire the way Altschuler is the class jock and plays basketball better than anyone else in the school. And I must say that he was pretty smart to get the whole class to make a hero out of Brutus and a heel out of Caesar. He's pretty good-looking too, but not as good-looking as the kid who played Mark Antony in the play. He invited Frankie Menlo to walk home with us today. Fred likes him.

You should choose your own friends though, not have some dopey mother who invites strangers to make our home their home.

sixteen

The next part isn't part of the story, so it is all right to skip over it. It's about what happened to me inside, after just a few weeks of being away from my real home and being in New York. I dreamed some of these things, and some of them are real. It doesn't matter which are which.

The very night Altschuler visited me in the apartment for the first time I dreamed a crazy dream. I was walking along the beach at home, my real home, and I never seemed to stop walking. The beach isn't that long in real life, so it wasn't my very own and familiar beach. It was an imaginary beach. But I thought it was the very one I used to take Fred to. At least I thought it was that beach in the beginning of the dream because naturally the little bastard was trotting along beside me. Otherwise I wouldn't have been at the beach. It was late in the year, and the only time

I went there then was to walk Fred. So the dream started out to be a recollection of the good, free walks I used to have with Fred. We started out OK. Maybe I was wishing that our walks now didn't have to be so short and always in the same places.

But after a while, as the beach got longer and longer and less the beach I knew but some other beach, *the* beach, the one that rims the beautiful ocean that people think about, the one without seaweed and jellyfish, poor Fred wasn't in the picture any more. I was. Just me. And the great expanse of sand and sea. And me running along that beach sometimes throwing myself in the sand and flinging it up in the air and sometimes splashing in the water that tickled my feet. I took off my clothes in the dream and then ran along the beach. I ran along the very rim of the tide, and it became windy and the sand blew all over me. I threw myself on the beach because the sand began to sting me as it blew against my body. Then I didn't know where I had left my clothes. I couldn't stand now because the wind was fierce. When I could stand up, the stinging was violent. How would I get my clothes? And what if I couldn't? Would I have to go back without them? Back where? I didn't know. I only knew that I didn't have what I needed to go on, to do anything. There was just me, and all I could do was lie there in the sand and try to bury myself against the fury of the wind and the awful stinging when I tried to get up.

I think the wind stopped. Or maybe I stopped it with some miracle which dreams make me think I have a supply of. Whatever the reason, I did get up, and I did walk back, and Fred did trot into the picture I was dreaming about, and the beach did get smaller, and I must have found my clothes, and it all came out OK in the end.

Except that in the morning I began to think. It was a Saturday morning, and the rule is that Mother and I play dead until it is inevitable that one of us gets up. That usually happens around the middle of the morning, though Fred and I have been awake for a few hours, just messing around in my room. And I think of all the reasons for my being here. I feel guilty as hell that I haven't thought of Grandmother for a long time. She's the only person I may ever know I didn't have to put on some big act around. She's the only person I could be myself with. My mother and my father don't know me yet. But I think of them more than of Grandmother, who will be the most important person in my life forever. And they aren't worth my not thinking of Grandmother. I love them and all that. They are trying to feel so goddamned responsible that they should be encouraged, but it's Grandmother who matters to me. And she is dead. And I'm forgetting her. Like a bastard. And I think of the beach in my dream and how I kept running farther and farther along it so that Fred and everything I knew and loved faded away. There was only me and that terrible wind and the stinging until I stopped it, which must have meant that I could go back to where I understood how everything fit together. Except I can't. She is dead. It has been many, many weeks now. There has been great cold, and snow, and she is back there in Massachusetts in that terrible box they put her in, in the ground. She is there, and it makes no sense that Grandmother and Fred and I are not sniffing around each other in our own ways. I cannot get buried in all this stuff happening to me now. The new stuff doesn't matter. As long as I remember.

It's dumb thoughts like these which occupy me while I try to stay in my room on Saturday morning. There is a limit though, and Fred reaches it when he gives me his special don't-blame-me-if-I-make-here look.

seventeen

For the next couple of weeks the most important thing to happen to me is that Altschuler and I get to be buddies, for a while anyway. He kept telling me that my mother was a real gas but also that he wasn't being friendly to me because Mother kept telling both of us that it was nice we were such friends. If the truth is to be known, we got to be buddies in spite of Mother rather than because of her. Altschuler, a native New Yorker, knew all kinds of places, and he took me to a lot of them.

Mother's house is right across the street from an Episcopal seminary. Mother never went inside the seminary. She likes it because it is pretty to look at. Whenever anyone came to visit her for the first time, she made a big thing out of the view she had from her living room, and from my bedroom too at the front of the house, looking out across a little park and into a dark chapel. She never thought of going over to the seminary, but Altschuler took me there a lot just to schmooze around. Some kid whose father got his call to be a minister late in life was a buddy of Altschuler's, and that kid had some buddies, so we messed around in the little park a lot. One of the seminary kids had a football, and we played touch a few afternoons. They wouldn't let me bring Fred. They said it was because they didn't want a lot of dogs to make all over the place. I planned in my mind to work out something for Fred later. Just to run around on some grass would make Fred happy. Besides, I had already seen about eighty wild cats jumping through their fence, and I'll bet they make all over the place when no one is looking.

One day Altschuler took me to the Holland-America Line pier, and we sat looking at the *Nieuw Amsterdam* for about an hour. Three sailors from the ship waved at us. They were just standing around, too. Altschuler told me that it took a day to land passengers, clean up the ship, and get ready for more passengers. It seemed very quiet on the ship. Only a few sailors were roaming around aimlessly, including the three who waved to us. Two guys in working clothes were doing something to some portholes. They were sitting on the same kind of thing window washers sit on when they are working on high buildings, a long platform fastened by ropes and pulleys to some place at the top. One of the workers was whistling.

"Where do you want to go the most?" Altschuler asked me.

I hadn't thought of going anyplace. I'd read about a

lot of places and seen a lot of things in the movies and on television about foreign places, but I had never thought of myself in connection with those places.

"It costs a lot of money to go places," I answered.

"Suppose you had money. Where would you want to go?"

Honestly, money is so important when you think of going anyplace, of getting on a ship like the *Nieuw Amsterdam* or in an airplane, that it seems goofy of me even to think about something like going to a place that is faraway. I mean, my father took me to Canada, and I'll go to visit Aunt Louise in Massachusetts this summer, I guess. But places that don't have something to do with some family person taking you there or being there and that's why you're going, places that aren't one of those places seem crazy for me to think about.

"What about you?" I say to Altschuler. "Where do you want to go?"

"I asked you first."

"That doesn't matter. Maybe we want to go to the same places."

"Come off it," Altschuler declares. "Either there are places you want to go or there aren't."

I have a feeling that Altschuler is making a production out of this for a reason, but I can't think what the reason is. Is he trying to decide whether I think about anything other than what happens to me from day to day or whether I think about other things and the other things aren't worth a second thought? Or is he planning to be a travel agent when he grows up? Or what?

"There is this place," I lie.

"Where?"

"Solo Khumbu," I say, remembering an old *National Geographic* of Mother's I had looked at last night.

"Solo Khumbu! What the hell is that?"

Then I act condescending and superior for several minutes and tell him that I thought everyone knew about Nepal, and Sherpas, and yaks and naks, and llamas and all the potatoes they eat, and all that stuff. Altschuler thinks I'm great, I can tell from the look on his face. So by mistake I ruin everything by throwing in some stuff about Thailand, which I had read about in another issue of *National Geographic* last night.

"How can rice shoots grow in a small country that also has Mt. Everest?" Altschuler asks.

"That's what's so great about Nepal," I tell him. Then I ask him right away where he wants to go the most. He tells me that wherever the Olympics are is where he wants to go. It doesn't matter about the place. He figures that he will get jobs where he can earn a lot of money in three years and then take off the Olympic year to go to the games, both the winter and summer Olympics. I think that I have just as good an imagination as Altschuler does but perhaps not his convictions.

Another place Altschuler takes me to one day is a section of several blocks along Sixth Avenue where wholesale florists have stores. We go into some of the stores and look as though we are buying for a big florist out of town, and Altschuler says that we would like to take samples of stuff back to our shop before we make up our minds about which dealer we will bring our business back to. Some of the stores give us each a couple of flowers, and we get about thirty stems by the end of the afternoon. Altschuler takes fifteen home, and I take fifteen. My mother tells me that it's unusual to see a gladiolus and a rose and a whole lot of other stuff mixed up together and where did I steal them. I tell her about calling on all the wholesale florists. She thinks that is funny. Fred wants to eat up the whole bouquet. I let him sniff it several times, and it kills him not to get a bite of it. After it is in a pitcher, he sits up in front of it and begs. He whines his nobody-loves-me whine when I won't let him have it.

"They'll make you sick, Fred," I say. "Flowers are to look at, not eat."

Then I remember he had a good time rolling all over the flowers they put on Grandmother's grave when she died.

"Maybe later, Fred," I promise. "When they stink more, you can roll in them then."

A very good place Altschuler took me to was the stamp and coin department at Gimbels department store. We went back three days in a row because Altschuler hadn't been there for several months and there were some stamps he wanted to look at. He told me about his collection, which is exclusively stamps of new African countries. One afternoon at his house I looked at the albums he had. I helped him with his new stamps, but he wouldn't let me do the actual licking and mounting. All I could do was line them up and hand them to him in the right order, like a slave.

One of the best things about going to Gimbels was going upstairs to look at all the puppies on sale. If I had the money I would buy every one of them so Fred would have buddies to play with. I'll bet that would go over big with you-know-who.

Toward the end of the second week, after we had been going home and doing something together for a couple of hours almost every day, when I met Altschuler after school, he asked me if I wanted to come over to his house all day Saturday.

"That's the day I always spend with my father," I tell him, "and Stephanie. That's his wife."

"Oh," Altschuler says.

But he says it as though he is mad at me.

"That's the only day I get to see him."

"Sure."

"Maybe you'd like to meet him. He'd be glad to have you come with us. I don't know what we'll do, but I'm sure he and Stephanie would like to have me bring my friend with me."

"Why?" Altschuler says.

"What do you mean, why? Because you're my friend, that's why."

"That's all right. Forget it."

"OK," I say. Now I'm mad.

"I don't have time to walk home today," Altschuler says. "I'm going to meet a friend later. See you." He gets on the bus just before the door closes. I don't even have a chance to get on. Altschuler leaves me standing there. I have to walk home alone, and I'm not sure why. I could run and catch the bus in a minute. It chugs along on donkey power, not like a regular city bus. I could catch it without any trouble at the first corner after it leaves the school yard. Why should I run just to do that? So I could find out why Altschuler decided to disappear in such a hurry, that's why. What's so important about not going over to his house on Saturday? I invited him to come with me. It's not as though I didn't want to see him. To hell with him. I'm not going to run after the bus.

So I walk home by myself. When I'm with Altschuler, there are certain ways we walk home, certain streets he wants to walk down, and some he tells me aren't worth bothering about. He's the expert, so we always go the way he says. Except for the first day I walked with him, we had never gone along Sixth Avenue on the side with the candy store, the one where the lady ran out to greet Altschuler. I decide that today I'll walk that way for no other reason than that it's a route Altschuler is always leading me away from. Besides, I like candy, and maybe I would like to buy something every now and then. Like today. When I get to the store, I go in. The same lady that made a big fuss over Altschuler is there.

"Hello," I say.

"Oh, it's Dougie's friend!" she says. "Where's Dougie? It's weeks since I've seen him."

I tell her I don't know where Altschuler is, and I look at the glass jars with an intensity I don't particularly feel, in spite of how I like candy. How come this lady is so wrapped up in Altschuler? She probably has a million customers a week. Does she get wrapped up in all of them? I'd better watch out. Or should I? She asks me what I like.

"Almost everything. I don't like licorice too well, but I'll eat it."

"No licorice! Just like Dougie! When he gets jelly beans, I always have to take the black out. It's no wonder he's your friend."

"How do you remember what everyone likes?" I ask. "With all the customers you have, it must be hard."

"Sure it is. So's life," she says. "When you've got a business, you remember things which help the business. What people like is very important in candy. Take, for example, if you were to buy Dougie a bag of candy as a present for his birthday, it would be important not to have black jelly beans in it. That's business, sonny. Business is giving people what they want. Remember that, when you're a big man doing a big business somewhere. It's advice like this you need. You'll grow up and go to college someday, and you'll learn business from books and you'll learn economics, and the *Wall Street Journal* will become your favorite comic book, and you might forget what a lady in the candy business told you. But *you* try to remember: Give the people what they want. That's business," she says, handing me a plate with fudge on it. "Try some. It's good."

I do. And it's good. I tell her so.

"What did you expect? I made it myself." She points to a row of jars. "That stuff I import from England. People in New York like to suck candy made in Europe. We got stuff here that tastes better and is cheaper, but New Yorkers like the English stuff. It's a cheap way to take a trip, you think?"

She tells me she forgot my name and I tell her what it is. She tells me I'm a good boy and I listen to advice.

"Poor Larry," she says. She takes a handkerchief from her apron pocket and blows her nose. "Such a boy!" She begins to cry, I think. "Like clockwork, every Friday, for years! Larry and Dougie would come in here for candy. Such a boy! You never knew him, if I recall. Him and Dougie were such a pair. Nice boys, not fresh like some kids I know. Always polite. Always please and thank you. That's manners. Kids today forget those things. Maybe it's because you boys are richer than most. Oh, I don't know. I like rich kids better than poor ones. Not that I don't like poor kids too. There's a lot of poor kids with fine manners, and very nice to talk with too. Oh, but there's something to be said for being rich. You boys start out with so much more. Count your blessings, sonny. Excuse me, I forgot your name."

"Davy Ross," I tell her.

"You're a nice boy, Davy. I can tell from the way you act. You're Dougie's new friend, aren't you?"

"Sure," I mutter.

"So where is he? Where's Dougie? He hasn't been in to see me since the last time you two passed by. Not once since poor Larry died. What kind of friend do you call that, who won't come to see me?"

"I'm sure he'll be in," I say.

"Davy, that's the right name, isn't it?" she says. "Promise me something. Tell Dougie that Mrs. Greene is a friend indeed. Promise you'll tell him."

"Sure."

"That's a good boy. Now choose what you want. For you there's no charge today."

I smile my greedy smile, and she laughs. I pick out some of Mrs. Greene's fudge and some caramels. She puts a lot of stuff in a bag for me, still laughing. "What did I tell you? Mrs. Greene is a real friend."

I save some of the fudge for my mother, but when I get home it is easy to see that fudge isn't what Mother wants this afternoon. On several days Mother works at home, doing this writing stuff she has to do for her job. I had forgotten that this was one of those days, and I'm happy that I had forgotten because if I had remembered I would have been thinking about it all day. She has stayed home to work about five times, including today, since I have come to live with her. On the other four days something awful happened when I walked through the door. It usually had something to do with Fred, who bothered Mother when she was trying to work. Mother gets a lot of pep for her writing out of the array of liquor bottles spread around the kitchen and living room. I can see right away that she is filled with plenty of pep today.

"Davy! Davy! Davy!" she says. "My precious lambie pie, my scrumptious strawberry tart, my delicious draught of apricot nectar! Come give Mummy a swell kiss."

I give Mother a kiss, practically falling on the floor because there's so much alcohol in the air around her.

"You must be working on a food account today," I say. Me, the comedian.

"What do you mean, my precious?" she says, sweeping me into her arms to kiss her again.

"All those food names you kept calling me." I laugh nervously. "I sounded like a three-course meal."

Mother doesn't think I'm such a comedian though. She is sitting at her desk, and Fred, of course, is running around both of us like a nut, begging for attention from me. She jumps up now and turns away from me.

"You've really got a lot of chutzpah, haven't you? Just like your father."

"What's chutzpah?"

"It's New York for nerve. You think you have all the answers."

"I'm sorry," I say. "I thought it was funny the way you called me all those foods. You must have been hungry," I continue, now nervous as hell. "Maybe you didn't have anything to eat today."

"What does that mean?" she says in a very loud voice, turning to me.

"Nothing, Mother."

"I think it means something. You *are* just like your father. I don't know why I let you see him every week. You're getting more like him every day."

"I'm sorry."

"With cracks about eating." She moves away. Fred follows her. I think he heard the word "eat," which he understands well, and thinks she is going to feed him. He gets mixed up in the hem of the long robe she is wearing, and Mother pulls it up from the floor.

"Get the hell off my robe," she says to Fred.

"Come here, Fred," I call. He comes dashing over to me. "I'll take him out, Mother." She doesn't answer, so I go out with Fred. I stay out about seven times as long as I would ordinarily, and Fred couldn't be more pleased. I walk him toward Fourteenth Street, which to Fred is like going to heaven since that's where the wholesale meat dealers are. When I have been out as long as I dare without there being a terrible scene about where I was for so long when I get home, I take Fred back to Mother's. The end of the Huntley-Brinkley news report is coming through loud and clear from the television set.

"Good night, Chet."

"Good night, David."

"Good night to both of you," I hear Mother call. "You bastards, I'll bet you don't spend your lives dog-sitting and kid-sitting. Good night, good night, get lost, both of you!" She turns off the television set and sees that Fred and I have returned.

"Good night, good night," she says, mimicking herself. "Good night, Chet. Good night, David. Do you suppose his mama called him Davy? What do you think, Davy?"

"I don't know."

"Of course you don't. If you cared for your mama,

you'd get right on the telephone and call that man and ask him if his mama called him Davy. That's what good little boys do. Isn't that right, Fred?" She bends down to Fred, who runs toward her and jumps up to lick her face. "That's a good doggie. Isn't our Davy bad? He won't call up the television man and ask him what his mama called him. What do you think, Freddy baby? Isn't our Davy a bad boy not to do that?" Fred gives her another lick. I don't know what she does then, but she must be pinching Fred or squeezing him tight because he suddenly yelps in pain and makes a snapping sound.

"My God!" Mother jumps up. "He tried to bite me!" Fred is confused and runs away from Mother.

"No, he didn't," I say. "You frightened him. You must have pinched him."

"He tried to bite me."

"It's because of what you did, Mother. You must have done something to him."

"I did not."

"He wouldn't have yelped unless you did."

I go after Fred. He has run into the bathroom and curled himself up behind the toilet. I bend down, and he growls at me, softly but certainly. I am surprised, so I don't say anything. I do put out my hand toward him, and he growls again and shows his teeth slightly. Fred has never done this to me before.

Finally I speak softly. "That's all right, Fred. It was an accident, Fred. No one is mad at Fred. I promise." Fred stops growling and looks at me very tentatively. "That's all right," I say. "Good Fred, good Fred." I put out my hand once again, and he lets me pat him. "Good Fred. Come to Davy." He uncurls himself from the back of the toilet and moves slowly out. On one or two occasions before, I think Fred has tried to walk on tiptoe, and he tries to do it again. I'm sitting there on the floor, so he marches right between my legs and jumps up to kiss me. We have a big love feast for five minutes. I tell Fred that accidents will happen and he shouldn't be mad at anyone. "Accident" isn't a word in Fred's vocabulary of course, unless he's smarter than even I think he is. I read somewhere that dogs have a thousand-word vocabulary as far as comprehension goes. Some people say that is crazy. All dogs do is respond to the tone of your voice. I don't believe that. I know dogs who are smarter than people. I know a specific dog who just may be smarter than my dumb mother with her dumb drinks and all that dumb talk about love and that crazy way she acts, one minute all love and kisses and the next minute like I just put a knife in her back. At least with Fred I know where I stand. Altschuler and my mother would make a great pair.

eighteen

The next day when I go out with my father and Stephanie, I am a regular gloomy Gus. My father doesn't pay any attention to me, but Stephanie can tell right away that I'm not the usual trying-to-please me. I already mentioned that Stephanie is schmaltzy. She has a cool outside, but if everything isn't hunky-dory she knows it in two minutes, and I can see her trying to find out what's wrong. I try to be jolly as hell and it's fake, and Stephanie knows it, so she works even harder, which makes me gloomier, and so forth. You get the picture. On some days it is not satisfactory to deal with people.

Today we go to a large department store uptown on the East Side in a part of New York people who live around Mother call fancy. Stephanie wants to look at some enameled pots she read about in *The New York Times*, and my father wants to get out of the store as fast as he can. He designs things like dinner knives, letterheads, lighting fixtures, door-knobs—all that kind of stuff. He is always talking about the low level of the public's taste and says that particular store goes out of its way to find ugly. Stephanie tells him he is mad because he can never find anything there he designed. He says of course he's mad for that reason and isn't that reason enough. It's not serious, the way my father and Stephanie talk. If I quoted them word for word, it would sound like an argument. It's not that at all. It's more like a joke where they both tell the truth to each other but without mean-ness. I wonder if my mother and my father were ever this way. Probably not. They could have been, I suppose. Would Father be a totally different person with Stephanie? Why does my father like Stephanie as a friend and not like my mother at all? I wonder whose son my father thinks I am. His? Mother's? His and Mother's? I don't usually give much thought to stuff like this, but because of the strange things on the day before with both Altschuler and Mother I feel sorry for myself, I guess. Especially since Father didn't say anything about bringing along Fred when he picked me up. And Fred knew right away when he saw Father that there was a real possibility that a lot of free food from Stephanie might be in the offing and that the alternative was to stay home with Mother, who loved him one minute and said some crazy things to him in the next.

The fact is that it's not Mother I'm thinking about so much that makes me gloomy. I'm used to her. Lady Mer-cury. It's Altschuler, and the way he ran away from me yes-terday just because of today. What a twirp!

"I think I won't stay with you for dinner tonight if that's OK," I say.

Stephanie practically falls through the floor. My father pretends that I said it looks like rain until I pursue the subject.

"You don't care, do you," I say, "about my not coming to dinner?"

"Of course we do, Davy," Stephanie says. "We care very much."

"Stop it, dear," my father says to Stephanie. Then to me, "You don't feel very well, kid? Is that it?"

Kid? What's this kid stuff? I think to myself. I don't always *say* what I want to say. Kid! It's like a movie, my father calling me kid as though I am an object, as though he wouldn't dream of being close to me or telling me things which are essentially private things, like the time a few weeks ago he told me about the Jewish cemetery and how Stephanie is Jewish. That was a personal and private thing for him to tell me. I know from the fact that I remember what he said that I was impressed with his having said anything to me about something like Stephanie being Jewish. Who the hell cares what anyone is? But if you talk about that stuff, it must be because it is important to you, and personal, or private, or whatever the hell you want to call it. I have so many thoughts about a lot of stuff lately. I used to have them before too, but with Grandmother there was a way to talk about something without actually coming out and saying let's talk about—well—why Mother doesn't come to see me very much. When I thought about this, and I thought about it a lot, it was possible to talk about how fast people could get around today, and Grandmother would say that the very rapidity which brings people together parts them as rapidly and things like that, which was our way of saying that even if Mother came to see me—and her—it didn't matter because she would disappear in two shakes anyway. So they could all stay away for all we cared. For all I cared. Who needs a lot of people who see you because they think they have to? Not me, that's for sure. I'd rather spend my time with Fred. There's a bastard who wants to be around me twenty-four hours a day. He wants *me*.

"I feel fine," I answer my father. "There's a lot of stuff I want to do at home, that's all."

Stephanie is fidgeting so much that I say they should forget what I said and that I want to have dinner with them. They stumble over each other to say I should do what I feel like doing. They each say that about four times.

"I want to be left alone!" I say. And I say it loud. We are still in the store, but we have moved from the enameled pots to the place where they have louvred blinds for windows. A lot of people turn to look at me. My father and Stephanie look as though I had tossed some enameled pots at them. I am surprised. I have raised my voice in a public place and in front of a lot of people, and to adults.

"I'm sorry," I say. "I didn't mean it to sound that way."

That's all right, that's all right, they both tell me. Maybe I should tell them honestly what I feel. Since they see me so infrequently, it's more important for all of us to be straight-forward than to be polite. The people who sell louvred blinds are looking at us with curiosity now. We have attracted a lot of attention from Saturday shoppers, so we leave the store. It's my fault. I know it is. I have upset the day, and that is dumb, and my father and Stephanie don't have anything to do with why I have ruined everything for them. And that makes me unhappy. They don't really have anything to do with me, do they? We see each other because we see each other. If I am teed off at something and it's my father and Stephanie I'm with, it's Father and Stephanie I am going to seem to be teed off at.

"Your father wouldn't take you to dinner?" Mother exclaims when I come home at six o'clock.

"Sure. They wanted to take me to dinner," I answer. "I didn't feel like it. That's all."

Mother is sloshed, it being a ritual with her that on Saturdays she can get sloshed earlier in the day than during the week. She knows that Father is supposed to keep me until late in the evening, and I have figured she does some serious gargling with Listerine around nine thirty every Saturday night so that when I arrive and Father takes me up to Mother's apartment, Mother will be ready with the I'm-a-nun act she puts on for Father whenever she has time to prepare it. She wasn't ready for me to come home at six, and not ready to see Father at all. Father understands this right away and doesn't linger to hear Mother's inevitable invitation to him to have a drink.

"Good luck, kid," he says to me. In a few hours I have grown to dislike the word kid, so I don't answer Father, or say good night to him either. He can really be a bastard when he's not even half-thinking about it. What a team they must have been, my mother and my father.

"If they didn't take you to dinner, you must be hungry. I'll rustle up something fabulous," Mother says in her dumb, sloshed tones.

"I'm not hungry, Mother."

"Of course you are."

"I'm not. Really."

"If your father and Stephanie didn't take you to dinner, you're hungry."

"No. I'm not."

"They didn't feed you, Davy. You've got to be hungry, sweetheart. I don't understand why they didn't take you to dinner, but that's beside the point. Davy's hungry. Stingy Daddy wouldn't spring for dinner. That's stingy Daddy for you. Mother's got a good idea. Mother and Davy will get all dolled up and go out to a posh restaurant and charge it to Daddy. Would you love that, sweetheart?"

"No."

"That's what I think we'll do. I'll get all dolled up. Mother will be the doll, and you'll be a regular wolf going out with an older woman. Wouldn't that be fun, sweetheart?" Mother is laughing away as though she has said the funniest thing in the world.

"I'm going to take Fred out," I say.

"They won't serve him in the restaurants I go to," says my mother the comic.

"I mean for a walk," I say.

"Go ahead. You can always get away from me, can't you, Davy?"

I tell her that I don't know what she's talking about, and she says I damn well do, and I tell her again that I don't, and she says I can run away with my dog all I want to but that when I come home I'll be coming home to Mother, and I'd better not forget that because it's Mother's life *which is being wasted...*

"You understand that, don't you, Davy? My life is being given over to someone else. I'm giving up everything, just as I always have. Your father. Now you."

I'm used to Mother sloshed, and I keep hearing about her lost life in one form or another, but she doesn't usually accuse me personally of being the source of her problem with life and all that. The closest she gets is Fred. It's Fred who is using up her life.

I take out Fred. It's a long walk. When I come home, it's seven thirty.

"Mother," I call when I get in. She doesn't answer. "Mother," I say again. I want to tell her that I'm sorry she is wasting her life. She isn't in the living room: "Mother!" I say once more. Her bedroom door is closed. I knock on it and go in. Mother is lying on her bed. She is dolled up. She is asleep too. She snores. Fred jumps at the side of the bed.

"No, Fred," I say. "Mother's tired. She's wasting her life for us, Fred. Right?"

I think Fred says "wrong," except that I know Fred doesn't speak English. Maybe he speaks German. Right? Who knows? Fred, I guess. And Germans.

nineteen

Altschuler doesn't speak to me very much the next week, and he doesn't suggest that we walk home after school. Miss Stuart, our English teacher, gets us talking together again. She thinks it would be a good idea if we put on our own version of *Androcles and the Lion*. Altschuler gets himself elected to play Androcles. He is still basking in his triumph from *Julius Caesar*, so whatever part he wants is his. Malcolm the slow learner seems a likely lion, but I decide that I want to be the lion. In the few weeks I had been in school I had learned who the three or four guys were besides Altschuler who had a following among the rest of us. I get to be the lion. I ask Malcolm to coach me on roaring, so there are no hard feelings. There doesn't have to be as much discussion about this play as there was about *Julius Caesar*. It is a simple story in which the slave Androcles does a good turn for the lion when he takes a thorn from his paw and the lion, in turn, remembers the kindly Androcles in the arena when the lion is about to eat him up. The important scenes are when the thorn is removed and when the lion recognizes Androcles. There's also a lot of philosophical junk in the play, but you don't have to pay attention to that.

"The play shows what a noble person Androcles is," Altschuler tells the class, "and how he gains the lion's eternal gratitude for all the noble things he does."

I tell everyone, "The play is about how seemingly dumb beasts have memories and the power of understanding. The lion recalls Androcles' acts. That shows how intelligent a lion can be. And how filled with gratitude."

"It shows that Androcles has been such a magnificent person that even a lowly lion appreciates him," Altschuler says.

"Don't think animals are so dumb," I tell the class. "I have a dog, a dachshund, and my dog is smart and truly understanding. Not just because he understands all these thousands of words I am sure he knows the meaning of, but because he knows people and can predict what they will do."

"It is men, not animals, who should attract our attention," Altschuler says, and he says it fairly loud so that even Malcolm will get what he is trying to say.

"Sure," I say, just as loud as Altschuler. "Men are great. But sometimes animals aren't as dumb as men think they are."

"Is that right?" says Altschuler.

"Yes, that's right," I answer.

"What makes you think that's the case?"

"Because I know it's the case."

"What? Because you have one dumb dog you think you know how a lion is supposed to think?"

"Why not? Besides, he's not dumb."

"Not as dumb as you."

Malcolm thinks that Altschuler is a hit playwright by this time and just about falls out of his seat laughing at Altschuler and me. Miss Stuart says she thinks we have gotten off the track and if we are going to put on our version of the play we should stop yelling at each other and start preparing the script. Since most of the guys don't have much to do in the play beyond being a gladiator or a wild animal, Altschuler and I have a script together in a couple of days by just working in the classroom, and we are ready to put on the play less than a week after Miss Stuart thought up the whole project. The school likes it. A lot of guys tell me they liked the way I licked my paw and cried like I was in pain, and a lot of them tell Altschuler that he was pretty funny when he came to the rescue and pulled the thorn out of my paw and again when he thought it was curtains for him. It's really everyone telling Altschuler and me how great we are. So that afternoon Altschuler says that maybe we should walk home together.

"Sure," I say.

"I'll meet you at the bus."

"Let's go to Mrs. Greene's candy store on the way home."

Altschuler looks at me for a minute.

"OK," he says, but without conviction.

We do meet, and we do go to the candy store, and Mrs. Greene tells him that he's a bad boy not to come to see her, and she kisses him, and she cries a little bit about Larry Wilkins, and she gives us some chocolate-covered marshmallows because she just made them. Altschuler promises he won't be a stranger, and she gives me a hug and tells me that I'm a good boy to bring Dougie back to her.

"She's goofy," Altschuler says after we leave.

"Sure," I agree. Neither of us believes it. We both like her.

We walk along for several blocks, talking about how great we both were in the play and maybe we should become actors because we both know how much money you can make if you are a successful actor.

"And you don't have to work too much either," Altschuler says. "I could make one movie a year and make enough money so I could get to the Olympics with no sweat at all."

I ask Altschuler to come to see Fred, and he says that would be fine. Mother is not at home, so dopey Fred has had a long day of snoozing and is in a state of ecstasy over our arrival. Altschuler and I take Fred out for a walk.

"I'm sorry about last week," he says.

"What do you mean?"

"About not being friendly."

"That's OK."

"The play makes up for it. We worked that out real well."

"Yes," I say.

"Together."

"Sure."

We are getting slurpy, we both realize. When Fred plops, it gives us something to look at rather than each other.

"That's a good doggie," I say to Fred.

"Good Fred," Altschuler says. "He smiled at me."

"Dogs don't smile."

"Fred can," Altschuler insists. "He was pleased that I complimented him on his dump."

"Maybe Fred can. He's unusual." I bend down to Fred. "Smile, nut." Fred licks my face. "That's not smiling."

"He does it only for me."

"Some people read human responses into animal behavior. My mother keeps telling me that."

"Your mother doesn't know what she is talking about."

"That's true," I say.

We go back to our house. Altschuler and I chase Fred around the apartment. Fred loves to duck under chairs and dart out from under them to see if we can catch him in a hurry. He wants to be caught, but he wants to be chased too. He has his favorite rag, and he uses that as though it is a prized object he knows I want from him. When he rests under a couch or a low chair, he is always looking to see in which direction he will be able to move to escape the feet pursuing him. It is fun to fall on the floor, down to his eye level, and threaten Fred with extinction unless he gives up the rag. Fred loves that.

I fall on the floor at one end of a couch in Mother's

living room. Altschuler falls to the floor, facing me. We are both threatening Fred, who is under the couch, with terrible consequences unless he gives up his rag. Fred is delighted. His eyes dart from Altschuler to me and back again, twenty times in less than a minute. Heaven! He is trapped, ready to be taken, rag and all. Both Altschuler and I reach out for Fred's rag and—zoom!—Fred has tricked us. He snatches it back and makes his way along the wall away from us for his getaway.

"Foiled!" Altschuler yells.

"By the smartest dog in Christendom!" I shout.

We laugh. I would have said that all three of us laughed except that Fred is at the opposite end of the room, far from us. Altschuler and I are lying on the floor, our arms still stretched out for Fred's rag. We laugh louder and louder. Fred has proved himself the smartest, the most uncapturable dog in the world. He is an animal! And what are we? Mere men.

Mine and Altschuler's laughing dies down, but we stay on the floor. I look at Altschuler, and we smile, sort of. And I'm not quite sure what happens now. I think we both intend to get up and chase after Fred, but there we are, lying on the floor, Fred peering at us from across the room, us half peering at Fred and wanting to chase after him again, but also not wanting to get up at all. I close my eyes. I feel unusual. Lying there. Close to Altschuler. I don't want to get up. I want to stay lying there. I feel a slight shiver and shake from it. Not cold though. Unusual. So I open my eyes. Altschuler is still lying there too. He looks at me peculiarly, and I'm sure I look at him the same way. Suddenly Fred jumps in between us. First he licks my face, then Altschuler's, and back and forth between us. I think that this unusual feeling I have will end, but in a minute the three of us are lying there, our heads together. I guess I kiss Altschuler and he kisses me. It isn't like that dumb kiss I gave Mary Lou Gerrity in Massachusetts before I left. It just happens. And when it stops we sit up and turn away from each other. Fred has trotted off, maybe tired of both of us by now.

"Boy," I say. "What was that all about?"

"I don't know," Altschuler answers.

We get up, and we avoid looking at each other. When our eyes meet, we laugh, but not like before.

Fred comes back and we horse around with him for ten minutes. Altschuler says he has to go home. I tell him he doesn't have to go home because of what happened on the floor. He says he knows that, and he also says that we were pretty great in the play.

"We're just a couple of great kids," I say.

"We sure are," Altschuler says. Then he sort of lunges toward me with his fists up like a boxer. We mess around for a few seconds, pretending we are two bantamweight tough guys. I mean very tough. I mean a couple of guys like Altschuler and me don't have to worry about being queer or anything like that. Hell, no.

twenty

The next day both Altschuler and I have to run for the school bus in the morning, so there isn't time to say more than hello until we are on the bus, and then nutty little Frankie Menlo insists that I sit with him and tell him about how I learned to be such a good lion.

"I went to a lot of zoos," I say.

"What ones?"

"Zoos all over the place. Haven't you ever been to a zoo?"

"Sure. But which zoos did you go to to learn lion behavior?"

"Actually I didn't go to any zoos," I tell him truthfully. "I remembered lion behavior from going to movies."

"Which ones?"

"How do I know which ones! Any movie I ever saw

with lions in it. I remembered those, and that's how I knew how to be a lion in the play."

"Did you see *Born Free*?" Menlo asks.

"Yes," I say.

"Is that the movie which taught you most about lion behavior?"

"I don't know. Maybe."

"It's my favorite movie of all time. That's why I asked you if that's the one you learned from."

"Sure. I guess I did."

"That is my seventh movie."

"What about the ones on television?"

"They don't count."

Menlo wants to know which parts of *Born Free* I liked the best, and I tell him I guess it's the end when Elsa comes back to show off her cubs. Menlo likes that part too, but his favorite part is Elsa riding on top of the wagon. We both like when Elsa is a cub herself, running around knocking stuff over and having a hell of a time.

"I'd like to own a lion," Menlo says.

I tell Menlo that he probably never will, not in New York anyway. He says that he will probably go to Africa to live. And then I tell him the truth about how I learned to be a lion.

"My dog taught me," I say.

"Your dog! What kind of lion can a dog teach you to be?"

"He taught me animal behavior."

"Animals aren't all alike."

"Enough alike."

Menlo looks dubious, but we are at school now, and it is enough that Menlo has had a talk with me on the bus to keep him in the power position I know he now has in the third grade.

Altschuler shoots off the bus in a hurry. There's no chance to talk during the day. He isn't at the bus after school. I walk home alone. It's Friday. I have to admit to myself that I want to talk to Altschuler about yesterday and all the goofy business on the floor. And then I don't want to talk to him either. Just as well it is Friday, and the weekend.

My father calls on Friday night to tell me Stephanie has a terrible cold, so maybe we should wait until Sunday to get together, if that's all right with me. I tell him to forget this weekend, and he tells me that he won't forget it at all, and I tell him that I don't mean what I said to sound unfriendly, that I understand about Stephanie's cold, and there's nothing wrong with missing one weekend every now and then. It's really OK, I keep telling him. And he keeps saying that it's awful. Then he tells me that with spring coming on he is going to take me and Stephanie and Fred to Montauk for a nice long weekend at the beach, and I'll love it there, that it is wild and desolate and Fred will be able to run and be as close to heaven as any New York dog can be. He assures me that the beach will be covered with smelly fish, just like at home in Massachusetts except that New York fish will be twice as big and ten times as smelly as those at home, and that maybe in another year or so he and Stephanie will even buy a house on the beach at Montauk and Fred and I can come out every weekend. This sounds pretty great, I must say, so at the end of the telephone conversation after I have told him about my lion performance and Stephanie has got on the phone to insist that I roar for her, and I do, and she roars back (she tries to make me feel as though I'm an over-achiever all the time), I'm laughing a lot.

"What did your father want?" Mother asks.

"Stephanie has a cold. I'm not going to see them tomorrow."

"Not see them! I've made plans, Davy! You see them every Saturday."

"It's Stephanie's cold. She feels lousy."

"So she feels lousy! What's that got to do with it?"

"Don't bother about me. I'm all right."

"What kind of mother do you think I am? Of course I'll bother about you. Your father may take his responsibilities lightly, but I don't. I wouldn't dream of leaving you alone for the whole day and the evening."

"It's all right, Mother."

"Who says?"

"I don't care, Mother."

"I do!"

Then she gets started on one of her solos, all about my grandfather and how he always teased her when she was a little girl and made fun of her every time she got a new dress, how my Uncle Jess used to tell her she was the world's most human dog, and about my father and all the years and talent she wasted with him and her family, which she mentions as though it's someone other than me, some third person entirely, some enormous burden she has carried day after day for the last four hundred and forty years. I know the end of these solos: a trip to the kitchen and an even more elaborate encore. In an hour or so Mother gets back to the problem though.

"What will I do with you tomorrow?"

"Don't worry about me."

"Of course I will, my precious," Mother says, giving me one of her warm hugs. She runs her hand through my hair and tosses it around. She can be a real lovable kid when she wants to be. "Mother worries about Davy because she loves him dearly," she says, her family suddenly no longer a burden but the thing that keeps her going. She's a hot-and-cold girl, there's no denying that.

I whip up some scrambled eggs, and Mother talks on into the evening of the good times we are having together. Fred eats Mother's eggs, and Mother thinks that Fred is the cutest animal in the world. I keep urging Mother to leave us alone tomorrow.

"All right, angel," she acquiesces. "Why don't you call your boy friend Douglas and invite him for the day?"

"No," I say.

"Why not? He's a nice boy. It isn't far, and you could have a lot of fun together. Call him up."

"No."

"You see him all the time. Why wouldn't you call him up and invite him over for the day?"

"He's busy."

"How do you know?"

"I just know."

"That's ridiculous. Did he tell you he was busy tomorrow?"

"He's busy every Saturday."

"Call him up, Davy. I won't leave you here alone."

"I don't want to."

"Then I'm going to call his mother myself."

I tell Mother not to, but she says that she knows what is best for me, and if I want to ruin her day that's entirely up to me. She will not go out to enjoy herself, even though this is one of the few occasions since I have come to live here that she has planned a whole day with friends for the express purpose of self-indulgence, *unless* someone is here with me. I tell her that I'll call someone else from school, and she asks me who, and I tell her about Malcolm, and she wants to know where he lives, and it is on Park Avenue somewhere in the Seventies, which is like another country. I even tell her about little Frankie Menlo, who must live nearer than Malcolm because we ride the same bus. When she hears how old he is, she decides I'm some kind of loon and starts to leaf through the front of the Manhattan phone directory. Mother calls Mrs. Altschuler and tells her who she is and invites Altschuler to spend the day with me. Mrs. Altschuler tells Mother that she has been hearing all about me and the lovely apartment we live in and what great friends Altschuler and I have become in a few short weeks. She accepts Mother's invitation for Altschuler without even asking him, so I can imagine how happy he is. Mother is pleased with herself and tells Mrs. Altschuler that it would be nice if the two mothers got together some-time.

"And Mr. Altschuler too, of course," Mother adds. There is a long wait while Mrs. Altschuler explains that Mr. Altschuler lives in Old Greenwich, Connecticut, with his present wife and their three children. I can tell right away that the conversation may go on for hours, as Mother starts to explain about Father's present wife too, and about how she, Mother, went without so many things while he was finishing his studies at Parsons School of Design, and how he then worked for years without contributing anything substantial to the family except when he started to make money and began to contribute his absence. The whole damn story pours out. The only thing stopping Mother from describing some of the grimmer details is that she has to stop every now and then to listen to the same story from Mrs. Altschuler. I take Fred out for his finals. When I come back, Mother tells me that she has just hung up, that Douglas is a wonderful boy, that Mrs. Altschuler thinks I'm a wonderful boy, and that Douglas and I are going to have a wonderful day together. He is going to stay over Saturday night, Mother tells me.

twenty-one

My mother does not come home until very late on Saturday, so she is still snoozing when Altschuler leaves on Sunday morning. It is the strangest, weirdest good-bye I ever had to say to anybody—somebody I saw every day last week, including Saturday, and will see every day this week. We horse around over some fried eggs I make and talk about Miss Stuart and stuff like that, but I have a new way of looking at Altschuler because of what we did together last night. Don't get me wrong, I'm not ashamed. There was nothing wrong about it, I keep telling myself. We got to talking about all the girls we had made out with. I told him about Mary Lou Gerrity and how I am more or less engaged to her, and that I haven't made out in New York because of being faithful to her. He told me about some girl named Enid Gerber he made out with at summer camp last year, and they are engaged too. That's how it happened.

"So I guess I'll see you on the bus tomorrow," Alt-schuler says.

"Sure," I say.

"What are you going to do this afternoon?"

"I usually hang around with my mother on Sunday," I say, "if she ever wakes up. She takes me to a movie or something like that."

"Oh, sure."

"When do you see your father?" I ask.

"I talk to him a lot on the telephone. Connecticut's a real drag."

"Oh, sure."

He is gone now, so there's nothing else to do except take out Fred and buy *The New York Times* when I see that Mother did not bring it home with her last night. I don't like to do that on Sunday because the paper is so fat. It's hard to manage both Fred and that big newspaper at the same time. I do all the things I usually do, and I even anticipate Mother's waking up and make coffee for her. You could call me a regular kitchen hand. But today it is not like before. I mean I feel weird. I want to call up that bastard Altschuler and have a good long chat with him. What about? I don't know. Do you have to have a reason? So I call him.

"What are you doing?" I ask.

He tells me that he is eating more fried eggs because when his mother heard that I made breakfast and the supper last night, she got worried. We both think that is pretty funny, and I say something to show how smart I am, about maybe he will end up crowing like a rooster, especially if they have chicken for dinner today, which I know they will because Altschuler already told me that his mother makes a chicken every Sunday. It's real dumb conversations like ours which give teenagers such a bad reputation for using the telephone.

"Well, OK," I say. "I just thought I'd call you up."

"What are you doing later?" Altschuler asks.

"I don't know. My mother isn't awake yet." Altschuler has the same problem I have, only in reverse. His mother never sleeps. He told me that if she gets three hours' sleep a night she thinks she's a regular Rip Van Winkle and wants to know what happened while she was out.

"I'll see you tomorrow then," Altschuler says.

"On the bus." I hang up.

And then I moon around. Today I don't care about *The New York Times*, not even the travel section, which I usually read first, or the business section, which I read because the biographies of smart businessmen are interesting and I think that maybe someday I'll read one about my father and how clever he is as a designer and how he got to be rich because everyone had to start using his doorknobs, or some knives of his, or something. I am glad Mother isn't awake. It is pleasant to be alone here with Fred, the only living creature I can speak to about Altschuler.

When my mother does wake up, I can tell right away that she won't be interested in a movie, so I give coffee to her and walk away without more than three or four words.

"What's the matter with you today?" Mother asks.

"Nothing."

"Why so quiet?" she says.

"I thought you wanted it that way."

"Where's Douglas?"

"He left after breakfast."

Mother makes a motion to silence me. She tells me about the magic power of sleep. She goes back to her room and closes the door. She sleeps the day away. I am alone with Fred. I decide not to call Altschuler again. Besides, isn't it his turn to call me?

There's nothing wrong with Altschuler and me, is there? I know it's not like making out with a girl. It's just something that happened. It's not dirty, or anything like that. It's all right, isn't it?

twenty-two

Altschuler and I see each other in school every day of the next week. We are friendly. As captain, he always chooses me to start on his side in the basketball games we play every day during the sports hour. I'm not as well-coordinated as Altschuler, and I don't move as fast as a lot of other guys, but I usually lob in a basket when I get the basketball. I just stand there and toss them in. I don't know why I should be so good at this, since I'm not a jock. I'm strictly average when it comes to sports except for swimming, when I'm on my own, and in track meets, where there may be a team but it's really everyone on his own. I've already told about what a great track star I was back home.

We don't have much to say to each other until Friday, when I run after Altschuler after school.

"Let's walk home," I say.

"No."

"Are you going someplace?"

"I want to get home early."

"We get there almost as fast walking as on the bus."

"All right."

We walk along together, and Altschuler is going so fast that I'm glad I am a track star.

"Hey, wait up," I say. "I wanted to talk with you. That's why I wanted to walk home with you."

"Sure," he says. He slows down. "I'm sorry."

Then I tell him there's no reason we shouldn't be friends like before. Does he agree with that? He says he does, but he doesn't sound convincing. I ask him if he thinks what we did last Saturday was wrong, and he says he doesn't know, that he hasn't thought about it much. I tell him that I thought about it all week.

We walk along without saying anything for five minutes.

"OK," Altschuler finally says. "I thought about it a lot."

"What did you think?"

"First, I have to tell you I didn't make out with Enid Gerber last summer. We talked about it, but we were afraid to. I lied to her too. I told her I make out with girls in New York."

"Do you?"

"No. The worst part is I wouldn't know what to do. You understand?"

I tell him I do. I also tell him that Enid Gerber probably would have helped him. He knows that, he says, but since he told her about all the girls he made out with in New York, she would have thought he knew what to do.

I tell Altschuler I didn't make out with Mary Lou Gerrity either, so we both have a big laugh over what big bull artists we are.

"How's Fred?" Altschuler asks.

"Come to see him."

"OK," he says. And he does, and Fred jumps all over him as though he is a king. Fred jumps on me too, but not so enthusiastically as on Altschuler. We take Fred for a walk. Altschuler knows a back way into the small park in the seminary across the street from my house, so we sneak into the park and let Fred run around free—off his leash—for ten minutes, until a guard comes by and gives us hell. Fred runs up to the guard to give him a big kiss, but the guard isn't impressed. I call to Fred and chase him, but he's sure this is part of a game, and he runs up and down on the grass, ducking into bushes to hide when Altschuler and I close in on him. In another ten minutes the guard is yelling that he is going to get us arrested. By this time a few seminarians in flowing robes have joined in the chase after Fred, who is enjoying himself thoroughly. One of the seminarians finally catches Fred and brings him to me. His robe is covered with mud, and Fred is licking his face. Everyone but the guard thinks Fred is funny. Altschuler and I hurry out of the park, warned by the guard never to come back again.

"You're a real Christian," I say to him, but only when

I'm far enough away so I'm sure he can't hear me. I'm a regular hero, you can see.

Altschuler and I laugh a lot over Fred's adventure. We go back to my mother's apartment and repeat about ten times how the guard looked, what he said, and how dirty the seminarian got catching Fred. We laugh each time we recall a moment. To tell the truth, it's probably the best laugh I've had since I got to New York. Fred finds us curious and looks from one to the other with surprised interest on his mug. I fall on the floor and give him a hug, which he likes so much that he goes into his purring-cat act. Altschuler bends to listen too, so, dopey me, I give Altschuler a dumb kiss. He looks surprised, and so do I, I guess. I get up right away.

"Did you ever drink whiskey?" I ask.

"I tasted it a few times. I didn't like it."

"I don't either," I say. "My mother sure does."

We both speculate that it makes a mess of peoples' lives but decide to have one swallow each from one of my mother's bottles. We have a few swallows each. I get woozy. So does he. I don't know how you could drink this stuff all the time, I say. Altschuler doesn't know either. He says that it certainly makes you feel warm inside though, doesn't it? I put some on my little finger to give to Fred. He licks it and sneezes. Altschuler and I decide to have a few more swallows and to drink water with it to see if it will taste better. It doesn't. We start to giggle like little kids. So I guess it makes you feel good, all right. After the next swallows we have gone from woozy to silly to downright dizzy, so we decide not to have any more. We laugh again about the guard in the park. We sit down on the floor with Fred. The next thing, we are sound asleep.

"My God," my mother yells, "what's going on?" Fred jumps up and down in front of her. She pushes him aside. Maybe it is twenty minutes since we went to sleep. Maybe more. It is dark outside. Probably more. Mother has come home from her office. Altschuler and I are spread out together on the floor of her living room. Fred has just hopped over to her from his perch, squeezed in between us, his nose stuck in our armpits because our arms have stretched across each other's back.

Mother's shouts and Fred's sudden jumping out of his position wake up Altschuler and me. Mother turns on a living-room light.

"Davy..." she says. "Douglas...What on earth...?" Altschuler and I get up.

"I don't understand, Davy," Mother says.

"What do you mean?" I ask.

"What were you boys doing on the floor in the dark?"

"Nothing. We fell asleep."

"Asleep? What the hell's wrong with you, Davy? It's not even six thirty, and you and Douglas are asleep on the floor in the dark!"

"What do you mean wrong?" I ask.

Mother sits down on the couch. She hasn't taken off her coat or anything like that. She sits there with this puzzled look on her face. She starts talking to herself about what she should do now. Altschuler says that if it's six thirty, he is late and has to leave right away. Mother looks at him blankly for a minute, then tells him that it is nice to see him. She smiles for a second and then asks him if he is all right.

"Sure," Altschuler says.

"Give my best to your mother," Mother says.

Altschuler now has a turn to look strange, and he tells Mother that he will. He shrugs his shoulders, and at the same time we both notice the bottle we took the whiskey from. It is standing open on a table in front of the couch. Mother sees it too, gets right up, takes off her coat, and carries the bottle to the kitchen, where I can hear her making herself a drink.

"I'll see you," Altschuler says.

"OK," I say.

"You don't think she thought anything wrong happened, do you?" Altschuler asks.

"Nothing did."

"Except the whiskey."

"We drink that like orange juice around here."

After Altschuler is gone, I ask Mother what she wants for supper. I offer to make this tuna-fish casserole I learned how to make from *The New York Times* a couple of weeks ago. She likes me to make stuff like that.

"Davy," Mother says, "I have to ask you a question."

"Yes?"

"What were you and Douglas up to on the floor when I came in?"

"We were asleep. That's all."

"Don't lie to me."

"I'm not."

"It's too improbable, sweetie. Boys don't lie around asleep on the floor in the middle of the afternoon."

"We were."

Mother takes a big swallow of her drink. "I can't stand being lied to!" She yells. "What were you doing on the floor?"

"I told you."

"Like hell you did!"

I go into my room when she yells again. She follows right along with me.

"Why won't you tell me what you were doing?" Mother demands.

"I told you."

"I mean what you were really doing."

"We drank some of your whiskey and fell asleep."

"Why did you do that?"

"Because..."

"Yes?"

"We wanted to see what it tastes like. What's such a big deal about that?"

Mother has her glass in her hand. She holds it out to me. "Here," she says, "have some."

"No."

"Why not?"

"I don't like it."

"You liked it before."

"No, I didn't."

"Why did you drink it?"

"For fun. To see what it tastes like."

"You know what it tastes like."

"Sure. But to see what kind of feeling you get from it."

"What happened?"

"We fell asleep."

Mother finishes her drink and goes back to the kitchen to make herself another. She doesn't come back though, and she must have finished it right away because I can hear still another drink being prepared. I also hear this deep moan coming from the kitchen. I follow her.

"Are you all right?" I ask.

Mother is sitting at this high stool she has in the kitchen. I can tell that she is crying and having a great time feeling sorry about what life has brought her to think about for the weekend. She holds her arms out to me, and I go over to her. She presses her hands to my face.

"Davy, Davy," she says, "truth."

I nod.

"Nothing...unnatural...happened this afternoon with you and Douglas, did it?"

"No," I say.

"Or ever?"

"What do you mean 'unnatural'?"

"I want the truth, Davy."

I back away from Mother. "What's so important about the truth? Why is it so important to know every little thing that happens in my life?"

Mother groans.

"You never knew what I did from one month to the other when I was living with Grandmother. She was the only person who cared what happened to me. You didn't. Father didn't. What makes you think you should know everything I do now?" I know the things I am yelling at Mother aren't what I would say to her if she hadn't asked me about this afternoon. I can't stop. "You never loved anyone in your whole life except yourself. You drink like you do because you can't stand yourself. Neither can anyone else."

Mother gets off the stool she is sitting on. She brushes against her drink, and it falls to the floor. Fred jumps back, and I'm glad for him that the glass does not break.

"You made a mess," I say to Mother.

She looks at me, her head shaking from side to side.

"I'll clean up your mess," I say. I reach for some paper towels from a rack over the sink. Mother grabs them from my hand and throws them to the floor.

"You... you..." she says as I bend down. She pulls me up.

"Davy..." She lets go of me and moves out of the kitchen. "I can't cope," she says. "I can't."

Mother must have told my father I was a lunatic when she called him on the telephone, because he is in the apartment in less than a half hour. I had gone to my room with Fred as soon as I had cleaned up Mother's drink. When Father arrives, he gets the usual warm greeting from Fred, a morose one from me. Mother keeps saying over and over, "I can't cope, I can't cope." Father looks around as though he were expecting the place to be damaged.

"The way the boy talked to me, David, I can't repeat it."

My father puts his arm around Mother. I just stand there.

"I can't cope."

"I'll talk to Davy, Helen," my father says.

"You only have him a few hours during the week. You don't know how he is."

I'm beginning to feel like a regular carbuncle. I was sorry I had said those things about Grandmother and all a half hour ago, but I'm not sorry now. Father doesn't know how I am! What does she mean by that?

"It's not just Davy," Mother continues. "The dog too. He's all over everything. I don't have a life of my own."

"Helen! Don't talk that way. Not in front of Davy."

"Why not?" Mother says. "You should hear the way he talks to me. I can't repeat the things he said."

Mother makes every move to encourage Father to ask her to repeat what I said, but he doesn't fall for it.

"Let Davy and me have a talk alone," Father says.

Mother looks around. "Alone? There's no alone here any more. Yes," she says, "you talk to him." Mother says she'll take Fred for a walk. I don't like this especially, because Mother doesn't walk Fred often, just when it's impossible for me to do it. Besides, she has just finished saying what a drag Fred is, along with me of course.

"Don't take Fred," I say.

Mother looks at me, and I know I have said the wrong thing.

"I mean," I say, "I'll take him out later."

"We're going out so you can have a talk with your father," Mother says. And that's the end of that. Fred doesn't care. He would go out eighty-two times a day if someone would take him. He runs through the door without even looking back at me.

My father asks me what has happened between my mother and me, and I tell him a lot of stuff about how she drinks so much and tries to run my life and know everything I do and when I do it and all that stuff. Just like I told her before, except now I'm calm, and I describe life with Mother in a way my father seems to think is funny. He says he knows exactly what I mean and that he is sorry Mother is the way she is, but that's the way she is, so what can we do about it? I say that I don't know, but it's pretty rough living with her. Father asks me if I would rather live with him and Stephanie. I hadn't thought of that before, so the idea surprises me.

"I don't know," I say.

"You like Stephanie, don't you?" he says.

"Oh, sure," I say. I realize that I like her a lot better than I like my father. He's no prize, running out and leaving me with Mother. I don't blame him though. I tell him I'm too young to make a lot of decisions about which parent I want to live with. Besides, neither is such a good catch, I say, after having had a great old girl like Grandmother to live with.

"But your grandmother is dead," Father reminds me.

"Sure," I say. "I know."

"About this other thing. Your mother was pretty upset on the telephone. She said something about what had been going on between you and a friend from school. What's that all about?"

"Nothing."

"Sure?"

"I don't know why she is so upset. We fell asleep on the floor this afternoon. Is that such a big deal?"

"I think she meant something else."

"Oh," I say.

"Is he a special friend, Davy?"

"Sure. Altschuler. I told you about him."

"I'm not prying, Davy," my father says, "so don't get mad. We don't talk about personal things much, but sometimes it can't be avoided. I guess you have a crush on your friend, is that it?"

"A crush?" I ask. I get red in the face. "I don't know." I can't think of another word. "I'm not queer or anything, if that's what you think," I say.

Now my father gets red in the face. "I'm sure you're not, Davy. I don't want to make a big case out of this. Your mother does though. She's an emotional person. She gets upset easily. She thinks you will end up … well, I don't know what lengths her imagination will carry her to." My father goes on to tell me that a lot of boys play around in a lot of ways when they are growing up, and I shouldn't get involved in some special way of life which will close off other ways of life to me.

"We only made out once," I tell my father. He laughs. So do I. He's OK sometimes, and he sure got the information out of me a lot less painfully than Mother could have.

Then Father talks a lot about how hysterical people sometimes get when they discover that other people aren't just what they are expected to be. He tells me there are Republicans who are always secretly disappointed when friends turn out to be Democrats, and Catholics who like their friends to be Catholic, and so forth. He says that such people are narrow-minded, he believes, and funny too, unless they become hysterical about getting everyone to be just alike. Then they are dangerous. They become religious bigots, super-patriots, super-antipatriotic, and do I understand? I tell him I think I do, but can't people learn to understand other people? He thinks they can, but only if they want to.

It has been a long talk, and I'm nervous about the time Mother and Fred have been gone. So I get up and go to the window looking out over the street. I peer up and down the street, but there is no sign of them until I see something dart around the corner at the dark end of the street. At first I suppose it's a cat because they run loose all the time, but I look again and see a woman, Mother, running, turning the corner too. The low dark thing is Fred. I can just make him out, working his way along the stone wall around the seminary. He passes under a street lamp, and I can see that he is dragging his metal leash with him. Mother is running after him, calling out, "Fred, Fred, here, Fred." I guess Fred thinks it is a game. He darts farther away from Mother. I throw up the window and am leaning out. I turn back to my father, who comes to the window.

"He'll be all right," Father says. "Your mother will catch him."

"What if she doesn't?"

"Sure she will."

"Fred is never off his leash on the street. He doesn't know how to act off the leash here in New York. I'm going down!" I scramble to the door and run out into the hallway. I jump down the stairs two at a time, but since I'm not used to that I go slower than I would ordinarily. It takes me half a second to get back to going down stair by stair. I get to the bottom. No more than thirty seconds all told from the window to the bottom of the stairs. And then I hear it. A big thud. A terrible, unnatural yelping. I throw open the door as a car filled with people speeds down the street. I see Mother running toward a place just opposite the house. "Fred!" she yells.

"Fred!" I yell. "Fred, Fred, Fred, Fred, Fred!" I keep repeating, "Fred, doggie, where are you?"

"Fred," Mother yells.

I run across the street. I can't see anything. My eyes are filled with tears. I bend down on the street. "Fred," I call. "Fred, doggie, where are you?" I close my eyes tight. The tears run out of them. I see Fred. He is under the very car I have thrown myself down next to. He is moving. I think he is moving. It's an unnatural, convulsive move. I've never seen him move like that before. I reach out to him. "Fred," I say. "Doggie," I say. "Are you all right?" I ask. I don't know why I ask that. I touch him. I can hear my father's voice behind me.

"Don't move him, Davy. He may have broken his leg. If you move him improperly that will make it worse."

So I don't move him. I keep my hand on him though. He stops making those convulsive motions. His eyes are wide open. I think he sees me. He sees me. I know he does. You see me, don't you, doggie? You're all right, aren't you, doggie? I can see a lot of blood coming out of his mouth. He's not making the slightest move now. "He's dead," I say. "He's not moving at all. I can feel him not moving."

My father crouches down. My mother does too. My father moves me aside gently. He reaches to touch Fred. He feels around, then draws Fred out. By this time there are about ten people standing around. One guy says he got the car's license number. Fred still has his eyes open, looking up at me. He looks all right except for that blood. Maybe he's just unconscious for a while. One man steps out from the people who are standing around. He says he can help. He touches Fred in a few places and says he is sorry.

If Fred is dead, how come he is still looking at me? Fred, you're not dead, doggie, are you? I pick up Fred and hold him close to me. I wrap my arms around him and rub him on the belly because I know how much he likes that. My mother is sitting down next to me. She is rubbing Fred too.

"He got away from me," she says. "He was doing his business, and he just pulled away from me. Poor dog. Poor dog."

The people standing around begin to move away now.

"We can take him to the doctor, can't we?" I ask my father. "Maybe he's just knocked out."

"No, Davy. He's dead."

We take Fred upstairs. I carry him. My father calls the A.S.P.C.A. to find out what we do now, and they tell him about the possibilities. My father asks me if I want to put Fred in a cemetery. I tell him that I want to keep him, that something will happen and Fred will be all right tomorrow. He says that it won't happen that way. I ask him why I have to decide now, and he says I just have to. I say that the only place I want Fred buried is with Grandmother. I know that's crazy, but Mother and Father don't laugh at me. They turn away from me and begin to cry, both of them. I look at Fred again. My dog. Then I cry too.

twenty-three

The only good thing about Friday is that my father spends the night at Mother's. He takes Fred to the A.S.P.C.A. to arrange his cremation, and when he comes back, he sleeps on the couch in the living room, right outside my room. I bawl a lot, so he doesn't get much sleep. He comes into my room and just sits on my bed. He tells me to cry all I want. I don't *want* to cry at all. But I keep waking up. As soon as I do and realize again that Fred isn't lying on top of my blanket or snuggled up around my feet, I get a sick feeling and say stuff about not believing what has happened.

"I'm sorry, Davy," Father says several times, "it did." Sure, I know it did. But I sure as hell don't want to believe it.

Finally morning comes. Mother hasn't slept much either. None of us wants to eat anything. Mother keeps telling me how sorry she is.

"I loved Fred," she says. "I didn't act like someone who loved him. God, Davy, I'm so sorry."

Her eyes are puffed up, and I know she has cried all night too. But I can't bring myself to say that it's OK and I understand. I don't. I understand that Fred is dead. I know what is happening to him this morning, and I want to be sick to my stomach. It is less than a day since we went to the seminary park and played games there. Now what is left of Fred is a lot of junk. Two of his rags. A hard blue ball he chewed on. A couple of half-eaten hide bones are on a shelf in the kitchen. I can't touch them, even to throw them away. I can't touch anything Fred touched. The whole world of Mother's house is Fred for me—what Fred could do, what he couldn't do, where he could go, and where not. Everything is Fred.

The next part is not clear to me. I go through several days. I do things I do every other day, but I don't remember what I do from one hour to another. Without Fred to walk, to come home to, to sleep with, to feed, to think about, to love—all that stuff—there isn't anything to do. So I just think.

Who's to blame? It's no one's fault. It just happened. Why does someone have to be blamed? I'm not trying to blame anyone. I am though. Why? Fred has died, and someone is to blame. I want Fred. I can't have Fred. Who says? The bastard who ran over him, that's who says. It's his fault? It's no one's fault. It happened. Someone did it. The man driving the car? No. Who else ran over him? No one. Then he did it? Yes...that is, no. Did Mother do it? No.

Not as though she sat down and did it, like making one of her drinks. She didn't do it as a positive act. How do I know? She didn't think how she was going to get Fred run over, if that's the dumb thought running through my head.

Since I was a little kid, I have been responsible for a lot of things, principally Fred. I couldn't have been more responsible than I was for Fred. Grandmother left me in complete charge of him. Look what happened. It isn't my fault. Whose is it? It wasn't Mother. He was doing his business. He pulled away from her. He was a speedy son-of-a-bitch when he wanted to be, and clever too. He thought it was a game. I could see that from the window. It was the kind of playful challenge he liked best. Was it the dog's fault? No! He was a dumb creature. It wasn't his fault! Maybe she should have watched him better. She could have held on to him better. He was only a little dog. It's her fault? No! Whose? I don't know. Not the dog's. Not hers. It just happ … she took him out because of me. She wanted to leave me alone with my father to talk. Is that why it happened? Yes, God, yes. It's my fault. Because of everything I did. It wouldn't have happened if it wasn't for me. It is too my fault! All that messing around. Nothing would have happened to Fred if I hadn't been messing around with Altschuler. My fault. Mine!

twenty-four

For weeks, six weeks in all, the only thing I can think about is Fred. I do other things. I go to school. Altschuler tells me several times that he misses Fred too. I thank him. I'm polite enough, but I don't want to talk about it, so I don't ask Altschuler to walk home with me, and I don't hang around trying to bump into him accidentally all the time, which is what I was doing before Fred died. I come into classes as late as I can so Altschuler won't get a chance to talk to me about anything important, and I run out after class like the original bolt of lightning. Altschuler isn't dumb, so we don't talk much after the first week. By the fourth week after Fred died, I try to find ways to avoid seeing Altschuler at all. Every time I look at him I am angry. For the first few days when I start to feel this way, I am angry at myself for having gotten mixed up with Altschuler at all. It doesn't take long before it's Altschuler

I'm mad at and not myself. It was that talk about making out with Enid Gerber and Mary Lou Gerrity that got us started. It was a bunch of lies, in other words. We would never have done anything if it hadn't been for those lies. Mine too. But mostly his, I think. They *were* mostly his. That's what led to all the trouble. Fred died because of some stupid lies about making out. It certainly isn't in my nature to queer around. I never did it before. If it hadn't been for Altschuler, I would never have done it at all. I can't stand the sight of Altschuler. I guess it gives me some pleasure for the next two weeks to think how much I hate Altschuler.

Six weeks pass, and we are playing baseball outdoors. I'm no athlete and certainly no baseball player, but New York kids don't have room to practice baseball anywhere, so in my school they are even lousier than I am. I get elected captain of this dopey team that goes to a lot of other private schools around New York to play. The first game is with another Episcopal school with an even worse team than ours, so we win the game by a dramatic score. Just about every kid who goes to bat for our side gets a home run. We have to stop the game in the fourth inning, because it is dark and our team has only one strikeout after each of us has been at bat twice during this inning alone. If we had gone nine innings, it would have been after midnight before the game broke up.

So the next day I am an important figure in the school. Frankie Menlo practically dusts off my seat on the bus on the way to school. It's ridiculous to shine like a star among these guys. In Massachusetts they wouldn't have been allowed to pinch-hit in a hurricane, and here they are on our first team. That I am the best player is comment enough on the rest of the team. I remember my grandmother was forever repeating that everything is relative, and now I know what she meant.

It doesn't matter though. For the first time in six weeks I begin to get used to life without Fred. I can see that life goes on without him, even for me—and this dumb baseball team I am the star of.

The next week we tie a nonsectarian school, but in a few days we slaughter some more Episcopalians. Altschuler is on the team too, but he doesn't shine as he did on the basketball floor, and he isn't nearly as good a hitter as I am. He tells me how great I am all the time, but I don't thank him when he says it. I don't know why. Except I do know why, so why do I say I don't?

The fourth game is the hardest. No score. Bottom of the ninth. Davy the Dazzler gets a home run, the only score of the game, and against a nonsec school. In the locker room afterward, everyone is yelling and screaming about what a great guy I am. They are also running around and snapping towels at each other. They have more energy here than they have on the field.

"Slugger Ross!" everyone is yelling. "Hooray for Slugger Ross!" The guys like to horse around like that. It's OK, I guess. As long as I remember I'm no great shakes.

Some guy snaps his towel on my backside when I am going into the shower. It stings so much that I turn the water on very cold to take away the burn. The water is like needles against my body. I like it a lot. I like the force pounding down on me, my eyes closed so I can get as close as I can to the nozzle.

"Great hit," I hear someone say at the shower nozzle next to me. I smile without opening my eyes. "Really great." He pats me on the shoulder. I open my eyes, and it's Altschuler taking a shower next to me.

"Get your hand off me," I say.

"What do you mean?"

"You heard me."

Altschuler takes his hand from my shoulder. He is smiling. When he sees that I am serious, he stops smiling.

"I just wanted to tell you how great you were," he says. "That's all."

"OK."

"What's eating you?"

"You didn't need to touch me."

"What the hell is the matter with you?"

"I don't like to be touched."

"Since when?" Altschuler says.

Altschuler shouldn't have said that. When he says it, it is like being clobbered in the stomach with a ramrod. "You're a bastard," I say.

"I don't know what's eating you."

"Don't you?"

"No."

"You should, you bastard."

The water is still pounding away at both of us. I guess

we are talking loud, but so is everyone else. They probably think we are just horsing around.

"We're going to end up a couple of queers," I say. "You know that, don't you? All that junk back there before Fred died. You know what happens, don't you?"

"You're crazy," Altschuler says. He shuts off his shower and turns to walk away. I don't know what gets into me. I grab Altschuler and pull him back to my shower.

"Like hell I'm crazy," I yell at him. Then I don't know what else to do. I have hold of Altschuler with one hand, so I raise my other hand and smack him across the face. Hard. He is wet and slippery, so it is easy for him to pull away from me.

"You sure as hell are crazy," he says.

I go after him again. "Don't you know what happened to Fred? Don't you know why?"

"It had nothing to do with us."

"It was because of what we did, you dumb bastard! That's why my mother was walking Fred that night. Because of us. Because of all that queering around."

"Shut up, Davy," Altschuler says. "You sound like a creep."

"I'm a creep all right," I say. "So are you!"

Altschuler hits me in the face then. Before we know it, we are slugging away at each other. Some of the guys have heard us now. They are standing outside the shower room. We are pushing each other. The floor is slippery, and I fall. He falls with me. We are banging at each other's heads and at our chests. I can see some blood running next to my head.

It is a rich red trickle which gets pink as the water from my shower reaches it and dilutes it. When Altschuler sees the blood, he pulls away from me.

"That's from your head, Davy," he says. "What happened to your head?"

I sit up and feel the back of my neck. My hand rubs my ear, and I can feel a split in the skin behind the ear. It doesn't hurt, but my hand gets a lot of blood on it in no time at all. By then Mr. Miller, who coaches baseball and a few other sports, in addition to teaching geography, has told Altschuler to turn off the shower and is kneeling there looking at me.

"What happened?" he says.

"I slipped, I guess."

Some of the guys laugh. When I look at them, no one says anything, which proves that being a two-bit hero has compensations. Everyone has clothes on except Altschuler and me, and I am thinking more about us, naked, than I am about the blood. We look, well, naked. When I try to stand, Mr. Miller has to steady me. He has also put a towel over my ear to stop the blood.

The next few minutes are confusing. I put on clothes. Mr. Miller takes me across the street from the park we had the game in, and a doctor puts a few stitches behind my ear, telling me I'm lucky I didn't crack my skull open. The cut begins to hurt a little, and I'm pleased to get out of the doctor's office and to get a free taxi ride home, courtesy of Mr. Miller. He goes upstairs with me to explain to Mother what happened. Mother thanks him, and Mr. Miller goes away.

When we are alone, Mother tells me she is sorry I have the cut and that she would not know what to do if anything serious happened to me and I had better watch out in the future when I take a shower. I tell her I won't fall again. Our words are clear to me. They are the first we have spoken since Fred died which are not about what happened that night. Not that we have spent all our time talking about the actual event. We have spent most of our time not talking about it—and obviously not talking about it. Mother hasn't been on her juice as often. She hasn't become a saint in two months, but she has managed to take only two or three drinks in the evening, no more. She has tried to interest me in the activities of the Reform Democratic Club of the Chelsea area of New York City. If I didn't know better, I would think she was a member. She is afraid to join though. She thinks politics is to discuss, not to do anything about.

Tonight she kisses me about eighteen times. She's a regular Florence Nightingale. By nine o'clock she has begun to feel the absence of Fred in our lives, so she has broken her rule about drinking in moderation. She falls asleep on the living-room couch. There is no Fred to walk, so I have nothing to do but go to my room.

When the telephone rings, I answer it. It is Altschuler.

"Are you all right?" he asks.

"Sure."

"I'm sorry about what happened in the shower."

"You are?" I say.

"Of course. I didn't want to hurt you. I didn't, did I?"

"I'm all right, I guess."

"That's good."

There isn't anything more to say, so we pause for a minute and say nothing. Finally Altschuler says he will hang up. I tell him that's fine with me, and we both hang up. Then I tell him to run along and screw himself. No one hears me. Except me.

twenty-five

My cut ear makes me the greatest hero our school has ever had. Most of the kids don't know, or forget, that I got the cut in the shower room. Every time I walk down the corridor this path is cleared for me, with kids looking at me on either side. Me and Moses, leading the people through the waters. I'm hopeful that the baseball season won't last too much longer. I feel like such a phony.

Fortunately there are only two more games. I can't play the first one. The second is against a team made up of boys living in Harlem. They are such good players that my real talent gets back into perspective, and we are slaughtered. Whoever said "fame is fleeting" knew what he was talking about, because the day after that game against all those black boys, I join the ranks again. Even Frankie Menlo has a hard time hiding his contempt.

I feel so happy about this turn of events I even ask

Altschuler if he wants to walk home from school with me. He says that he does. When we come to Mrs. Greene's candy store, we go in, and she starts to cry because we have ignored her so long, and then she starts to give us one piece of about every candy in the store. It is almost like it was several months ago before everything happened.

"Don't you ever buy anything from her?" I ask Altschuler after we were out on the street again.

"I used to. At first, when I went in with Wilkins. After a while she wanted us to sample everything and tell her how we liked her candy. She used to say it was market research."

"My mother talks about market research," I say. "At the advertising agency where she works, people spend millions of dollars to find out what other people think of products."

"Not Mrs. Greene. Just hundreds of pieces of candy." We both think Mrs. Greene's way is the preferred way, and I plan to tell my mother a few facts about market research that evening.

When we get to my corner, it is awkward. This is where I used to ask Altschuler to come and see Fred on the times we walked home together before. We stand there for half a minute and don't say anything. Finally Altschuler says something about how strange it must be to go in and not have Fred jump all over me.

"Yes," I say.

"He was really something," Altschuler says. "The way he would squirt in a little puddle when we came into your apartment. Did he do that when it was just you coming in too?"

"Yes," I say, and it really hurts me to remember Fred's dumb little puddles. I would get angry at him, because I knew my mother could tell what Fred had been up to, no matter how well I tried to clean up his squirts. They were only little ones. I would tell Fred how terrible it was to get so excited. I think he used to tell me how terrible it was to leave him alone for so long.

"What did you do with Fred?"

"What do you mean?"

"Is there any place you can go to visit him? Like people?"

"No," I say. "He is cremated. I decided that."

"Wasn't that hard?"

"Of course it was." I am angry at Altschuler. Why does he want to talk so much about something like this? "You're kind of morbid, aren't you?"

"I'm sorry. I thought if there was a place, you and I could go there sometime. That's all."

"Oh," I say. And I'm not angry at him anymore.

We tell each other good-bye. When I get to Mother's apartment, I am too much aware that Fred is not there to jump on me. If I were still a little kid, I guess I would have gone into my room and cried for a half hour, especially since Mother is not home. But between what happened to Grandmother in the fall and how I created an ocean by crying so much about that, and what happened to Fred a few months ago and I cried a lot about that, I don't have it in me to cry too much from now on. Instead, I feel sad, not for myself but for the two guys I loved, Fred and Grandmother. What do you do if you feel sad and you don't want to moon around all the time? You do things, I guess, just as I did things with the baseball team. It was because of becoming a big fake hero in school that I was able to stop thinking about Fred all the time in the first place, wasn't it?

The first thing I do is straighten out my bureau drawers, which are a mess from having my things stuffed into them. That takes me twenty minutes. Then I rearrange the pots in the cabinet in Mother's kitchen. In New York cabinets, pots have to fit inside other pots, because there is no room for each pot by itself. Mother doesn't bother to arrange her pots correctly, so there are always a few sitting on the stove and on top of the refrigerator. That takes about ten minutes. Then I think that I will arrange all Mother's books alphabetically by author, until I remember that some of them don't have regular authors. They're things like dictionaries, and an encyclopedia in one book, and a whole lot of other things which make that plan difficult. It takes ten minutes to decide I won't do that. The next thing I do is put all the spoons in the spoon part of the tray, the knives with the knives, and so forth. Those are about all the things I can think of to do, and only an hour has passed. I figure that Mother will be home soon and there will be plenty to talk about with her, but she calls to say that she will be very late and I should make my own supper.

I call up Altschuler. I tell him that he can have supper with me if he would like to, but his mother won't let him. I also tell him that I'm sorry I have been acting so unfriendly.

"That's OK," he says.

"Would you like to go to the Museum of Natural History on Saturday?"

Altschuler asks his mother if he can go out with me on Saturday, and she says it's OK, so we make a date to meet at nine fifteen at the corner of his street. I call up my father, but he isn't home. Stephanie is. I tell her that I'm going to the museum with Altschuler on Saturday, so they don't have to make plans to see me.

"Is that the boy . . ." Stephanie starts to say, then doesn't finish.

"He's my friend. Did my father tell you something?"

"No, Davy, only that he was a best friend, if that's the same boy."

"It is."

"That's great," Stephanie says. "I'm glad you have a good friend. But can't we see you anyway? I'd like to. We'll take you and Altschuler to lunch. You'll save your money that way."

Stephanie is a real practical lady, so I tell her that it will be fine to take us to lunch. She says we'll go to a place near Central Park called Reuben's, because it has delectable sandwiches. She tells me how to get there and that we should come at twelve thirty.

I write down the directions, making a note on the paper: *Saturday, May 11, 12:30, Alt., Stephanie, Father, and me.*

twenty-six

The sandwiches at Reuben's are delectable, and so is the strawberry cheesecake. It's probably the best lunch I ever had. Altschuler thinks so too. Afterwards, Stephanie and Father walk with us to the zoo in the park. When we come to the seal part, I remember about how Fred honked at them when he came, so I don't enjoy the seals. The whole zoo turns me off this time. I had liked it before, in spite of what Stephanie had said about animals in cages. That morning at the museum, Altschuler and I hadn't seen too many things before we had to go to lunch, so we decide we'll go back there for the rest of the afternoon. Father tells us that he'll see us around, and Stephanie asks if she can walk with us through the park. Altschuler likes Stephanie, so he is delighted to have her with us. Stephanie talks to us as though we are people, not kids and something apart from other people, so I guess most kids would like her anyway. What I mean is that she treats us like equals. Not too many old people do.

When we get to the museum, Stephanie says that she enjoyed meeting Altschuler. She gives me a big kiss right in front of all those noble words about Theodore Roosevelt and nature and conservation that are cut into the stone there. Altschuler tells me that between my mother and Stephanie, if I ever get a choice, I should live with Stephanie. Before I know it we have moved into the stuffed North American animals part. I look for the place I remember from before and to the case with the coyote in it. The coyote is still there, and I hurry to it. Altschuler asks me why I am going so fast, but there isn't time to explain. The animal is standing in the exact position he was in before. When Altschuler catches up with me, I point to the card which still says that coyotes make good pets and are tame if they are caught young. Nothing has changed.

"Isn't he great?" I say to Altschuler.

"I guess so," he says. But he isn't enthusiastic about the coyote.

"Hello," I say to the animal.

"Come on, Davy," Altschuler says. "Don't be crazy."

"Hi, friend, coyote friend," I say. I press my hand against the case at the point nearest his muzzle.

"Davy, it's stuffed," Altschuler says.

"This one is different," I say. "Look at him."

Altschuler looks very close at the coyote. He tells me that it is a nice coyote but that I shouldn't talk to stuffed animals.

"What the hell do you mean I shouldn't talk to stuffed animals? Look at that animal. Look into his eyes. He sees me. He understands me."

"Those eyes are glass. Everyone knows that."

"They aren't," I yell. "This coyote is a strange creature. He understands. I know he does."

"He's dead and stuffed! Are you nuts?"

"He's a pet. He was somebody's pet, and he will be a pet forever. Why don't you get lost in some dinosaur bones if you don't want to look at the coyote?"

"You're nuts to think stuffed animals understand you."

I grab Altschuler's arm. "Don't keep telling me I'm nuts. I don't like it."

"Tough," he says, and he pulls away.

"I think I don't like you again," I yell.

"Would you rather talk to a stuffed animal than a person?"

"It's not..."

"Look at it." Altschuler points to the coyote. "What is it if it isn't a stuffed animal?"

"It's a pet."

"He's dead, Davy," Altschuler says.

"He looks friendly, don't you think?" I say.

"Sure."

"Let's go," I say.

We go back out into Central Park. I tell Altschuler I'm sorry that I got angry at him. He tells me I shouldn't be sorry. He's not, and he got angry at me too.

"Life should be beautiful," says Altschuler the kid philosopher.

We walk all the way back home from the park. We walk on Ninth Avenue, past a lot of meat markets, fruit and vegetable markets, bars, and the Port Authority Bus Terminal. And we talk.

For the first time in my life I talk about some of the things I am afraid of that I think about.

"Look, Altschuler," I say after a few minutes. "I think we have to talk about this queer business."

"OK."

"That was a very peculiar night, wasn't it? I don't want you to think I've done that before."

"OK," Altschuler says.

"Is that all you can say? I mean, didn't it upset you?"

"Sure it did. But it didn't feel wrong. Did it to you?"

"Look what happened."

"What happened to Fred had nothing to do with what we did."

"Maybe it did."

"Go ahead and feel guilty if you want to. I don't."

"You don't, really?"

"No," Altschuler says.

"I guess the important thing is not to do it again," I say.

"I don't care. If you think it's dirty or something like that, I wouldn't do it again. If I were you."

"Maybe if we made out with some girls, we wouldn't have to think about, you know, the other," I say.

"I guess so. I hope I find one who won't laugh at me."

"Me too," I say. "Especially the first time."

"After the first it will be easy."

We don't say anything for the next few minutes. It is a warm spring Saturday, and a good day to look at all the junk on sale in sidewalk stands along Ninth Avenue.

"I guess some day we'll be old, like our parents," I say.

"I hope not like my parents," Altschuler says.

"Me too." I laugh. "My mother, she's really something. I can never tell whether she's going to be my big buddy or a regular witch. She's either slobbering all over me or ready to boot me out of the house. How she feels depends on liquor mostly."

"How my mother feels depends on who's around," Altschuler says. "If it's me, she screams and yells all the time. If someone else is around, she acts like the people in television commercials. Just nice people. My old man is another story. I don't know what he's like. I don't see him often enough to know him. I guess he's got his own life."

"I think I know my father a little," I say. "Except he seems more or less absent to me. When we see each other, everything has to be arranged. You know what I mean?"

"At least you see him," Altschuler says.

"I don't want to be like my parents either."

"Who do you want to be like?" Altschuler asks.

"Me," I guess. "And guys like my grandmother. There was a great old girl. She was real stiff by nature, but she had respect for me, and I respected her. It was the same way with Fred too. We respected each other."

"I respected Wilkins," Altschuler says.

"I guess we could respect each other," I say. "Do you think so?"

"Sure," Altschuler says.

REFLECTIONS

ON THE

40TH ANNIVERSARY

OF

I'LL GET THERE.

IT BETTER BE WORTH THE TRIP.

———————————————————

We Got There.
It Was Worth the Trip

BY BRENT HARTINGER

Wow, what a ride.

I'm not just talking about John Donovan's book, *I'll Get There. It Better Be Worth the Trip*. I'm talking about how much the world has changed in the forty-one years since it was published in 1969.

Now, after all these years, we've finally arrived at the "there" referred to in the title.

Where is that exactly?

I'll get to that, but first let me point out that John didn't just write a terrific, surprisingly timeless book. He founded a genre.

The genre of gay teen literature started, as both genres and movements usually do, with a single book: the one you now hold in your hands. Incredibly, it was the first teen novel to deal openly with the theme of homosexuality.

Since I'm—*ahem*—slightly more than forty-one years old myself, this genre, and all the many social changes it represents, has happened entirely within my lifetime.

Heavy.

John's remarkably prescient novel came a mere two years

after Robert Lipsyte's *The Contender* and (especially) S. E. Hinton's *The Outsiders* completely upended the genre of young adult literature, which had previously offered mostly only idealized notions of childhood and held that children's books should teach by example, offering young readers the paragon of the virtuous teen. Instead, this new wave of teen books highlighted flawed, confused, and very human characters, and embraced the realism and social consciousness that had long since invaded the rest of the arts.

In short, these new teen books were doing what good literature has always done: responding to and commenting on the major issues of the day. More importantly, they were relevant to the lives of actual teenagers, speaking to them not in a preachy, instructional way, but in a personal, intimate one. Not surprisingly, this was also the start of a massive shift in reading habits where more and more teenagers started actually buying and reading teen literature rather than skipping directly to adult books—a trend that has kept accelerating until now.

I'll Get There... doesn't have quite the same level of emotional realism as *The Outsiders*—in part, because the main character is himself emotionally repressed. But its subject matter was more daring—and is, even now, more controversial—than anything you'll read in the Hinton book. If *The Outsiders* was a cataclysmic earthquake that changed the entire literary landscape almost overnight (and it was!), *I'll Get There...* was a glacier—unchanging and motionless at first glance, but the start of something unstoppable.

The book opens on the death of the main character's

grandmother, who has been caring for him since he was five years old. Now the rest of his family, including Davy's mother, have to decide where he is to live—and this is pretty much as good a description of the feelings of gay teenagers as I've ever read now, but even more so in the 1960s: a sense of dislocation, a feeling that you don't quite fit in anywhere, that you don't really belong—not to mention the feeling that decisions being made for you by adults aren't necessarily in your own best interest.

But, of course, death isn't really about endings; it's about change. As the saying goes, the fire comes ripping through the trees, wreaking havoc, but also transforming the forest into something new, and planting the seeds for more changes yet to come. Sure enough, Davy's life changes dramatically, just as the life of almost every gay boy or girl changes in his or her teen years—generally the time that a person not only comes to terms with his or her own homosexuality, but also untangles the even more difficult puzzle of how to merge that self-perception with the perception of him or her by others.

Almost every person spends his or her teen years navigating the treacherous waters of identity formation, but unlike gay kids, most heterosexuals don't do it completely alone; they don't do it in a world where plenty of adults and other authority figures are telling them blatant lies about who they are; and if they make a mistake, the stakes usually aren't nearly as high.

(This is why I'm always amused when people accuse me of writing my 2003 gay teen novel, *Geography Club*, solely to further some kind of political agenda. The truth is, I thought, as I'm sure John did, that it would make a terrific story. Who doesn't love the story of an underdog? And trust me, very few people are more of an underdog than a gay teen. It's frequently the case that the whole world really *is* against them: their friends, their family, their society, and even their religion.)

With the death of his grandmother, Davy moves in with his tempestuous, alcoholic mother—an untenable living situation that is leavened only slightly by his touching relationship with his father, his mother's ex-husband, the only other person in the world who understands what it's like to live with his unpredictable mother.

But Davy's closest relationship, by far, is with his dog, Fred. Given that he even makes friends with the stuffed coyote at the Museum of Natural History, this is a pretty good indication of an emotional disengagement with other human beings.

On some level, even Davy knows that it's not enough to just love dogs. He has a dream halfway through the book. In John's perfect thirteen-year-old patois, Davy tells us the dream isn't important to the story, that we can skip right over it if we want. Unreliable narrator that he is, we ignore him, because we know instinctively that we're about to hear something that's key.

And we absolutely do. In the dream, Davy is running down a beach that is at first familiar, but soon becomes some place new and different. Before long, even Fred gets left behind, and Davy is all on his own. Then he's naked and being buffeted by a violent wind and stinging sand, and it's all he can do to will it to stop. Eventually he does, and everything is made right again. Or is it? When Davy wakes up, he realizes that it's already too late to go back to the familiar beach of his grandmother's house. His old life is dead and gone, and the only way left is forward, into the unknown beach, a place of wind and stinging sand—a place where Fred can't come.

In other words, the author is telling us that things are going to get a lot worse for Davy before they get better. (And he's also telling us: whatever you do, don't get too attached to that dog! If you've read children's literature at all, you know, as a general rule, dogs in children's books almost never fare well.)

Which leads us to what makes this novel particularly notable for its time—why we're still talking about it all these years later: Davy's relationship with his friend Douglas Altschuler—referered to simply as Altschuler. It's a pretty good tip to the reader that Altschuler is going to seriously shake things up in Davy's life when he rewrites the ending of *Julius Caesar*. "Life is filled with surprises," Altschuler says. It's no coincidence that Altschuler is dealing with a life-transforming death of his own—that of his former best friend, Larry Wilkins.

When Davy and Altschuler's simple friendship turns into something "more," John cleverly has it be initiated by Fred himself, who licks both boys' faces, back and forth, until they finally kiss each other. Fred knows the score.

This being 1969, and planet Earth, reality must eventually intrude on their innocent little love affair. Reality is represented very realistically by Davy's mother, who catches the two of them asleep together on the floor.

When she demands to know what's really going on, Davy replies, "What's so important about the truth?"

The truth does eventually come out—and it has its usual serious consequences. That's the scary thing about change: once it starts, you have no idea how far it will spread, how much havoc it will wreak. In Davy's case, it's the death of Fred. The reader knows that the dog has fulfilled his literary function and, therefore, it was time for him to go, but try telling that to Davy, who is heartbroken and blames himself for the death, for daring to want more than just a dog for a friend.

But even now, things are never anything but realistic in the world of *I'll Get There. It Better Be Worth the Trip.* When Davy's father learns what's going on with Altschuler, he turns out to be surprisingly understanding. It seems that he is all-too-familiar with the intolerant and narrow-minded.

In the end—in the last few pages, in fact—Davy (and, it seems, the author, who has been very circumspect until now) finally gets the courage to talk about the "queer" issue.

It's impossible to overstate how melodramatic the whole conclusion to this story might have played in the hands of a less gifted writer. If you're curious, watch the ridiculously over-the-top final scenes of *The Children's Hour*, the 1961 film version of the Lillian Hellman play about two female teachers accused of lesbianism.

There are no similarly simplistic answers in *I'll Get There. It Better Be Worth the Trip*. The book ends on a hopeful, but ambiguous note. Wherever the "there" of the title is, Davy hasn't arrived yet. How could he? It wasn't possible in the world of 1969, not for a thirteen-year-old boy.

But with this simple emotional truth, John was still far ahead of his contemporaries, not just in children's literature, but in other entertainment mediums. A year after John's book was published, in 1970, movie audiences could see *The Boys in the Band* (based on Mart Crowley's 1968 play). The work has its own kind of emotional truth, but unlike *I'll Get There. It Better Be Worth the Trip* (and like *The Children's Hour*), *The Boys in the Band* is decidedly backward-looking, all about defeatism and self-hatred. This wouldn't be the first time that teenagers, and the books written for them, would be far ahead of adults.

Meanwhile, we wouldn't really see significant non-homicidal fictional gays on television until the 1972 television movie *That Certain Summer*. In 1967, CBS ran a documentary that featured real-life gay men, but none dared to show their faces—they were filmed in shadow, and one was famously interviewed from behind a potted plant. Correspondent Mike Wallace kept the status quo firmly in place by dutifully informing the viewer that gay men are "incapable of a fulfilling relationship with a woman, or for that matter with a man."

Talk about John Donovan being ahead of his time! Sure, the author or artist who is the "first" to break through with a theme or topic often gets a lot of attention for his or her work. But how often is that work truly the "best" on that theme? John's was absolutely one of the best children's books published in the 1960s—and the best children's book about homosexuality for many, many years to come. But while the book was well received in 1969, at least in literary circles, few recognized its true import—except perhaps its many homophobic critics, who somehow sensed it was a sign of things to come.

This was John's second big achievement: opening the door for more books on the topic, works like Isabelle Holland's provocative *The Man Without a Face* the following year, and the lesbian-themed teen classic *Annie On My Mind*, which didn't hit the scene until 1982.

Things had changed a lot by 1991, when I tried to sell the first draft of my own novel that would eventually become *Geography Club*—but they hadn't changed *that* much. I was told again and again by editors that, as much as they liked the book, there wasn't any market for it: schools wouldn't buy it because it was too controversial, and libraries and bookstores wouldn't stock it because it was too much of a "niche" market (in addition to being too controversial). A few editors took the book to acquisitions—and were told by the accountants all the things that other editors had been telling me.

I had one editor take me to lunch in order to tell me, "We don't have any slots on our list right now for books with low sales projections." This took me aback, not just because *I* didn't project the sales of my book would be low, but also because it sounded like they sometimes *did* publish books that they didn't think would sell—but that all those slots just happened to be full up at the moment!

Later, I landed an agent, Jennifer DeChiara, who literally promised me that she would sell the book (she's since told me that she's never made that promise again, and she never will). But she had no better luck than I'd had on my own. She once told me that we'd been rejected by a total of seventeen editors—a figure that I once cited to an audience during a joint talk she and I were giving. The second I said that, she looked over at me and said wryly, "Oh, you were rejected by a lot more than seventeen editors—I just told you that to soften the blow!"

The editor who did finally buy it, Stephen Fraser at HarperCollins, had to move heaven and earth to buy the book, but it all paid off the in the end. Within two weeks, it had already gone into a third printing, and there was soon a play and movie version in the works.

The conventional wisdom about gay teen books—that there was no market for them—turned out to be flat-out wrong. So much for conventional wisdom.

Better still, my book was part of a massive wave of other gay teen books, many of which turned out to be "surprise" bestsellers too. Some were edgy, some were genre, some were funny, and some were literary—and many were downright excellent, the undisputed "best" in the teen canon.

Which brings us to "now." What did I mean at the start of this essay when I said we had arrived at the "there" that

John refers to in the title of his book? It's not that anti-gay prejudice is gone—not by a long shot, although we've finally entered an era where anti-gay bigotry must be preceded with some variation of, "I don't have anything against gay people—some of my best friends are gay!" That's something, I suppose.

Still, the era of "gay teen books" is over—has been over for several years now. Ask any editor. We're now in the era of "books where the characters happen to be gay." A character's homosexuality is usually no longer the central "problem" for the main character—the thing that's not resolved until the last few pages, or never resolved at all, as in *I'll Get There...*, because it couldn't be resolved in the world of 1969.

Instead, a character's gayness is usually simply something that reinforces whatever the book's central theme happens to be, the other thing that has to be resolved. It sounds like a small shift, but it's not. It's huge.

By the same token, books don't get rejected out-of-hand by publishers anymore if they have a prominent gay character (although good luck getting them into Scholastic or any of the other major book clubs!).

Anyway, this changing of the genre is absolutely not a bad thing. In fact, it reflects the experience of actual gay teenagers. Let me be clear: being gay is usually still a challenge. But it's not the issue that it was. For one thing, resolution is now at least possible, maybe even likely.

At least in the U.S., we no longer live in the world of *I'll Get There. It Better Be Worth the Trip.*, because actual gay teens no longer begin their own stories completely alone. At the very minimum, they now know there are other gay people in the world—that other kids are going through exactly what they are going through. The Great Lie that's been told to gay and lesbian teens for centuries—that they're the only gay person in the world, the only person who has *ever* felt like they do—has been exposed. The truth is out. And it's out, in large part, because of John and all the books he inspired.

Remember what Davy's wise old grandmother told him: that it's better to be part of a winning team than to win all by yourself?

If the genre of gay teen literature was a sporting event, John was on the winning team. It was a relay race of sorts, and I'm thrilled and proud to have personally carried the baton for one brief leg of it.

But let's give credit where credit is due: it was John who started this race in the first place.

Brent Hartinger is the author of many novels for kids and teens, including the gay teen paranormal thriller, Shadow-walkers, *coming from Flux in 2011. Visit him online at www .brenthartinger.com.*

The Trip of a Lifetime

BY MARTIN WILSON

As a teenager growing up in Alabama in the late 1980s, I knew I wasn't like most of the other boys around me, with their raging libidos, confident swaggers, and often harsh insistence on their male-ness. In retrospect, it is obvious why this was so: I was gay. But I didn't realize it at the time, or perhaps I didn't want to admit it. I was too young to know what or who I really was. It didn't help that there were no role models walking around in plain sight.

Now, *role models* is not a term I am fond of—it seems pat, preachy, even sentimental. But for gay kids, especially, role models are crucial. If you don't see anyone like yourself—be it on television, in a book, or even next door—then it's hard to make sense of what makes you different. The only gay people I had come across—as far as I knew—were effeminate and prissy. Obvious types you might say—not that there's anything wrong with that. But because *I* wasn't like that, then I thought there was no way I was gay, despite countless crushes on male classmates, fascination with other boy's bodies, and complete disinterest in the female anatomy. It wasn't until after college that I admitted to myself—and to others—that I was gay.

Times, for many teenagers, have changed drastically. Nowadays, gay teens can see mirror images of themselves all over the place: in movies, on sitcoms and reality shows, in the news, and of course in books. Indeed, the gay YA novel is now commonplace, offering an abundance of titles each year, everything from "high lit" to frothy fun. But it wasn't always this way—and certainly not in 1969, when John Donovan published *I'll Get There. It Better Be Worth the Trip*. Donovan's editor, the legendary Ursula Nordstrom, knew what a groundbreaking and controversial novel *I'll Get There...* would be. As she wrote him in a letter, "We're going to meet a lot of resistance to this book and we will be eager to fight that resistance as intelligently and gracefully as possible."

I only found out about the novel after reading a review of *Dear Genius: The Letters of Ursula Nordstrom*, in which many of her letters to Donovan appear. As an aspiring writer, I thought the realm of YA was largely off-limits for the kinds of stories I wanted to tell—that is, stories about gay adolescents. So I was shocked that this book—about a gay teenager in New York City, published way back in the dark ages—actually existed. How had I never heard of it?

I was determined to track down a copy. I checked online and saw that the novel was out of print. Then I combed the shelves at used bookstores, to no avail. I finally ordered a copy from an out-of-print bookseller over the Internet. A few weeks later, my copy arrived, a battered ex-library edition that to this day still maintains that wonderful dusty smell of an old library book.

Reading *I'll Get There. It Better Be Worth the Trip.* was a revelation. Because not only was the novel about a young gay teenager struggling with those first pangs of confusion and homosexual attraction, but it was also—to my surprise—a beautifully written book. What had I expected? Probably not much more than a mediocre, white-washed novel full of preachy lessons and corny and outdated world views. Sadly, even at that time I wasn't aware of how sophisticated and brilliant so much of young adult literature actually is. For some reason I only recalled books where teens said "gee whiz" and "shucks" and always learned a valuable moral at the end. I certainly don't remember coming across curse words in YA books. Sure, there were a few Judy Blume books that I had stolen peeks at, the sex scenes in *Forever* and the period talk in *Are You There God? It's Me, Margaret.* But the Blume books seemed like an exception, a daring anomaly in a field of idealized versions of adolescence where less-seemly aspects of adolescence have no place. That this wasn't even the case didn't matter. My perceptions of YA lit were all that mattered, enough to discourage me from reading, much less writing, such work. So, surely such a novel couldn't deal with homosexuality in a convincing and compelling way. And surely this out-of-print novel couldn't be, well, art.

It was a joyous occasion to realize that I was wrong on both counts.

Davy Ross is an appealing narrator, both sardonic and sensitive, projecting a toughness that masks an almost-heartbreaking loneliness. Davy's loneliness is relieved mostly by his lick-happy dachsund, Fred, perhaps one of the most vividly evoked dogs in all of literature. But then, at his new school, Davy meets Doug Altschuler, the class jock, and slowly but surely the two become friends—and, eventually, much more.

And what of this relationship between the two boys? *I'll Get There. It Better Be Worth the Trip.* isn't an explicit gay love story by any stretch. Davy and Doug have a few homosexual encounters, which are treated tastefully and subtly in the book—rolling around on the floor, roughhousing that leads to kissing. While not explicit, these encounters are not sugarcoated and glossed over. Donovan honestly evokes Davy's constant state of confusion, and also his fears about what has occurred between him and his friend: "There's nothing wrong with Altschuler and me, is there? I know it's not like making out with a girl. It's just something that happened. It's not dirty, or anything like that. It's all right, isn't it?" But even by the end of the novel, Davy is still confused by what is going on inside himself. Much like I was at that age, and even on into my twenties. Whether you're growing up in Manhattan or Tuscaloosa, Alabama, realizing you're a homosexual is rarely something one arrives at without pain, bafflement, and fear. Isn't adolescence awkward enough when you're a heterosexual, attracted to whom you're supposedly supposed to be attracted to? How, then, do you account for the fact that your eyes are drawn to the football player's butt and not the head cheerleader's? At thirteen, Davy still has no clue that he is gay, even if the reader realizes that he most likely is. In 1969, this is totally understandable. At age thirteen, again, this is totally under-standable. Actually, it's still understandable today, at any age and in any place.

I think this is what some contemporary critics of Don-ovan's novel have a problem with: That Davy isn't out and proud at the end of the book. That the novel isn't some "go shout it on the mountain" affirmation of homosexuality. Sadly, such critics miss the point. Davy is on a journey, and by the end of the novel he has grown and matured in count-less ways. But he's still a kid. He has a ways to go. I mean, look at the title of the book. He'll get there one day—what-ever "there" is.

Davy, though mystified by his urges and feelings, is a kid with his head screwed on tight. He sees through a lot of the crap that adults say or do. He sees his flawed par-ents, and he resolves to be a better person, to not make the mistakes they have made. He's honest and humane. And he's taking things one day at a time. He'll realize his true feelings soon enough, and he'll face them with honesty and integrity. This, I think, is what contemporary teenag-ers today can take a way from this novel: Don't be afraid to be true to who you are, but get to know yourself first. Get comfortable with yourself. Love and respect yourself. Everything else will follow in time.

I first read Donovan's novel when I was an adult, openly gay, comfortable in my own skin. But I now wonder: what if I had come across this novel as a teenager? Would it have made any kind of impact? I like to think it would have given me some comfort, knowing I wasn't, in fact, alone in the world. There were other boys like me out there. And seeing yourself reflected in the culture as a visible, strong hero of a story is as important today as it was in 1969. Anyone who picks up *I'll Get There. It Better Be Worth the Trip.* today—forty years after it first made its appearance—will still find this lovely novel to be a relevant and compelling story of a boy trying to find his place in the world.

Martin Wilson was born in Tuscaloosa, Alabama. He received a BA from Vanderbilt University and an MFA from the University of Florida, where one of his short stories won a Henfield/Transatlantic Review Award. His debut novel, What They Always Tell Us *(Delacorte Press, 2008), won the Alabama Author Award for best young adult book. The novel was also a finalist for a Lambda Literary Award, an Indie Next Selection, an ALA-ALSC Rainbow List Selection, and a CCBC Choices Book. He lives in New York City. Visit him at www.martinwilsonwrites.com*

Taking the Trip with Davy and Altschuler, and What Happened Along the Way

BY KATHLEEN T. HORNING

Perhaps by today's standards, John Donovan's *I'll Get There. It Better Be Worth the Trip.* seems a bit tame, but when you consider it in the context of the times in which it was published, it is downright revolutionary. It was published just a few months before the famous Stonewall Riots erupted on June 27, 1969, noted today as the catalyst for a national gay liberation movement.

During the months Donovan was writing his novel and at the time it was first published, gays and lesbians had even fewer rights in the United States than they have today. Homosexuality was still classified as a psychological disorder by the American Psychiatric Association, and homosexual acts were considered a criminal offense in every state except Illinois. Most gays and lesbians had to go underground in order to survive. They were largely invisible in real life and most certainly invisible in youth literature. In retrospect, it's amazing that such a book was written, let alone published.

It started with a query letter from Donovan to editor

Ursula Nordstrom, the head of the Department of Books for Boys and Girls of Harper & Row (now HarperCollins), asking if she would consider publishing his novel about "buddy-love." Perhaps Donovan put out those initial feelers to Nordstrom because he thought that, as a lesbian, she might be more open to a gay novel, and might better understand the issues. Speaking about the publication of *I'll Get There. It Better Be Worth the Trip.* in a 1979 interview that appeared in *The Lion and the Unicorn*, Nordstrom said: "I had for years said that I wished someone would write a book that would give just a hint that there could be a romantic feeling between two persons of the same sex. It happens to almost everybody when they're growing up, a crush on a teacher or something, and they outgrow it or they don't outgrow it."

In her years at Harper, Nordstrom had established a solid record of publishing cutting-edge children's novels, including *It's Like This, Cat* by Emily Cheney Neville, which won the Newbery Medal in 1964. Like *I'll Get There...*, it also deals with a disgruntled teen named Davey, living in New York City, who feels a growing disconnect from his less-than-perfect family. *It's Like This, Cat* and the groundbreaking *Harriet the Spy* by Louise Fitzhugh, published by Harper a year earlier, helped to usher in what was then called "New Realism"—novels for young readers that depicted life as it really was, rather than as adults wanted children to believe it was. New Realism was quickly replacing the familiar and comfortable romanticism of childrens books published in the first half of the 20th century, and, although popular with young readers, it was not entirely accepted by the literary establishment in the children's book field in the 1960s.

It's Like This, Cat was also an early example of the newly developing genre of young adult literature, books featuring teen protagonists, aimed at teen readers. As those born in the post-World War II baby boom entered adolescence, there was an increasing recognition of the importance of the teen years, and publishing books specifically for this new generation of teens was seen as an important way to meet their educational and recreational needs.

Nordstrom responded enthusiastically to Donovan's query letter, saying that she had been waiting to publish a good book involving "buddy-love problems" for a long time, and that she would be happy if he would be the one to write one successfully. She received and accepted the manuscript six weeks later, on August 5, 1968, and she and Donovan worked to get the manuscript into final form by September. Several of Nordstrom's editorial letters concerning the book were published in *Dear Genius: The Letters of Ursula Nordstrom*, edited by Leonard Marcus (Harper-Collins, 1998).

We don't see Donovan's side of the correspondence, but from Nordstrom's letters to him, we can see that there was considerable talk about how a children's book with a gay theme might be received. Nordstrom expected there would be a lot of resistance to the book, and assured Donovan that they would be ready to fight it as "intelligently and gracefully as possible." With that in mind, she asked his permission to send a copy of the manuscript to Dr. Frances Ilg, Director of the Gessell Institute of Child Development at Yale University, hoping for an advance quote to put on the jacket. In her letter to Dr. Ilg, Nordstrom writes that this would mark the first book on the topic for young readers, and they were worried about adults who might stand in the way of the young readers who would read it with "some recognition and some relief." Dr. Ilg provided a three-sentence testimonial that was used on the book jacket:

> A moment of sex discovery is told simply but poignantly in the life of a thirteen-year-old boy through his relationship with a friend of his own age and sex. It is how he absorbs this experience that becomes the key to what will happen next. Davy is able to face the experience and make his choice.

Nordstrom's concerns about resistance to the book turned out to be largely unnecessary, at least in the library world, where she feared the book would meet its harshest critics. It was widely and positively reviewed in the professional library journals that recommended books for purchase by both school and public librarians, and it received starred reviews in two of the most influential library journals: *Kirkus* and *School Library Journal*. Interestingly, it was reviewed— and recommended—twice by *Catholic Library World*, once for Catholic school libraries and once in a review section for young adults, where it was labeled "HIGHLY RECOMMENDED FOR YOUNG ADULTS AS WELL AS ADULT READERS."

These reviews show a great deal of sensitivity and appreciation for Donovan's depiction of the boys' relationship. In his *School Library Journal* review, Michigan librarian Bruce L. MacDuffie wrote that the story provided a "...steady confirmation that self-knowledge is strength, self-respect renewable, [and] mutual respect central to all relationships." The unnamed reviewer for *Kirkus* concluded "It's a very moral (and discerning book) about a boy, not a moralizing or exploitative fix on a problem."

Outside the library community, reviews were mixed. Although it received glowing reviews in *Book World* and *Saturday Review,* the critics writing for the *Atlantic Monthly* and the *New York Times Book Review* both found it unsettling, with the latter oddly referring to Davy's affection for his dog as "bestiality." The review in the *Atlantic Monthly* was the only one, however, to offer strong criticism of the boys' relationship, saying that "...the application of grammar school jargon to corruption and passions is neither natural nor comforting." These two reviews were the exception. Overall, the book was both highly regarded and recommended for young readers at the time it was published.

Since then, critics have been less kind to the book, pointing out that it falls into the same trap many early gay teen novels did, which was to punish the main character with a car accident leading to death or serious injury. (In Davy's case, his dog was hit by a car.) Some have also criticized the book for depicting gayness as a choice or suggesting that being gay is just a passing phase, and they worried that this would misinform young readers. Many critics have also zeroed in on the guilt Davy felt after "making out" with his best friend Altschuler, especially when he feels responsible for his dog's death as a result.

None of them, however, commented on Davy's age as being significant—he is just thirteen, with a fairly naïve view of the world, and it is his view of the world that informs the novel, as he is groping his way in the dark and into adolescence. He takes his cues from the people around him: from his late grandmother ("...a great old girl. She was real stiff by nature but she had respect for me...") and from his unstable, homophobic mother who completely overreacts when she learns Davy shared a romantic kiss with his best friend. And from his father, who is divorced from Davy's mother. In a heart-to-heart talk, he reassures Davy that what he and Altschuler did was normal, a phase that he would outgrow. More significantly, however, he gives Davy an important message about self-preservation:

> Then Father talks a lot about how hysterical people sometimes get when they discover that other people aren't just what they are expected to be. He tells me there are Republicans who are always secretly disappointed when friends turn out to be Democrats, and Catholics who like their friends to be Catholic, and so forth. He says that such people are narrow-minded, he believes, and funny, too, unless they become hysterical about getting everyone to be just alike. Then they are dangerous. They become religious bigots, super-patriots, super-antipatriotic, and do I understand? I tell him I think I do, but can't people learn to understand other people? He thinks they can, but only if they want to.

Even by today's standards, this is a powerful and radical message for a father to give to a son who might be gay.

Another aspect of the book that's usually ignored by critics is Davy's love interest, Altschuler. He's also thirteen but he's just a little bit wiser than Davy, and certainly more comfortable with who he is. Davy looks up to Altschuler and even calls him "the kid philosopher" after Altschuler tells him, "Life should be beautiful." When Davy confronts him after his dog is killed, Altschuler tells him that he's crazy, that it wasn't his fault that the dog died, and it wasn't because of their "queering around."

> "Go ahead and feel guilty if you want to. I don't."
> "You don't, really?"
> "No," Altschuler says.
> "I guess the important thing is not to do it again," I say.
> "I don't care. If you think it's dirty or something like that, I wouldn't do it again. If I were you."

The book concludes with the two boys repairing their friendship by agreeing to respect each other. The ending is wonderfully vague and open to interpretation. We don't know if Davy and Altschuler will get back together in the romantic sense. After their last conversation, it seems plausible. Actually, Donovan has brilliantly constructed the novel so that it offers one message (it's just a phase) to the audience who needs that message in order to find the book acceptable, and another (be true to yourself) for those who needed to find the recognition and relief Ursula Nordstrom had hoped the book would offer to some young readers. I like to think Davy and Altschuler found that beautiful life together, or at least started out on the same journey to get there.

Today's books with gay, lesbian, bisexual, and transgender teen characters shows that both society and young adult literature have come a long way in the forty years since *I'll Get There. It Better Be Worth the Trip.* was first published. They feature more diversity in terms of themes and characters; original storylines, both comic and tragic; and overt expressions of sexuality and gender. We've gotten here in a large part thanks to the pioneering efforts of John Donovan, and to the courage of his publisher and the librarians who served as a bridge rather than a barrier between the book and its readers. They showed us that life for gay kids not only could be beautiful, but should be, and that it was a trip worth taking.

Kathleen T. Horning is the director of the Cooperative Children's Book Center of the School of Education at the University of Wisconsin-Madison.

About the Author

John Donovan was president/executive director of the Children's Book Council from 1967 to the time of his death in 1992. In that capacity, he worked tirelessly for the promotion of children's literature. He also used his influence to encourage publishers and educators to work together in finding reading materials for the classroom. He was the author of six books for children (two picture books and four YA novels).

About Stacey Donovan

The author of the young adult novel *Dive*, Stacey Donovan is a novelist, editor, writing coach, and ghostwriter. She also writes nonfiction and specializes in Social Media. Visit her at www.donovanedits.com.